“The amulets are gone.”

She grabbed his hand to pull him through the crowd on the dance floor, but the moment Olena touched him, Cale felt a lightning bolt of desire. He knew they had to get out of the club, away from the magic spell that was affecting them both. But he wanted to stay.

He wanted to bury his hands in her hair and kiss her hard and long. The thought of her tongue dancing with his made him instantly hard. Shivers of hot desire made his flesh quiver. Cale needed her so much, he could hardly breathe.

His brain told him it was magic making him feel this way. But in his heart he knew the desire had already been there.

He had to taste her. One taste would sate him. But even as he reached for her and crushed his mouth to hers, Cale knew with this mistress of the night, one kiss would never be enough…

Dear Reader,

The moment I finished writing the previous book, *The Vampire's Quest*, I knew I would want to return to the European Otherworld city of Nouveau Monde. And I knew exactly who my next story would be about—sultry vampiress Olena Petrovich.

I love writing strong, independent women, and Olena is definitely that, having been on her own for a couple of millennia. But I also love that she's vulnerable and wants to find that perfect someone to spend many more years with. So who better to throw into her path but a sexy British Interpol agent named Cale Braxton. Oh, and did I mention that he's human?

How is that going to work?

I hope you keep turning the pages to find out.

All my best,

Vivi Anna

Come visit me at www.vivianna.net or drop me a note at vivi@vivianna.net. I love hearing from all my readers.

VIVI ANNA

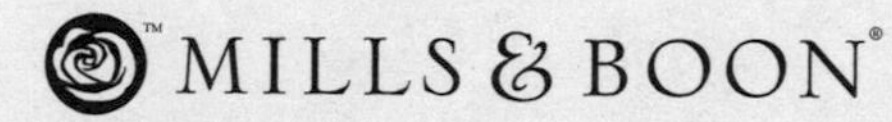

First published in Great Britain 2010
Harlequin Mills & Boon Limited,
Eton House, 18-24 Paradise Road, Richmond, Surrey TW9 1SR

ISBN: 978 0 263 88777 8

89-1010

Harlequin Mills & Boon policy is to use papers that are natural, renewable and recyclable products and made from wood grown in sustainable forests. The logging and manufacturing processes conform to the legal environmental regulations of the country of origin.

Printed and bound in Spain
by Litografia Rosés S.A., Barcelona

A vixen at heart, **Vivi Anna** likes to burn up the pages with her original unique brand of fantasy fiction. Whether it's in the Amazon jungle, an apocalyptic future or the Otherworld city of Necropolis, Vivi always writes fast-paced action-adventure with strong independent women that can kick some butt, and dark delicious heroes to kill for.

Once shot at while repossessing a car, Vivi decided that maybe her life needed a change. The first time she picked up a pen and put words to paper, she knew she had found her heart's desire. Within two paragraphs, she realized she could write about getting into all sorts of trouble without suffering any of the consequences.

When Vivi isn't writing, you can find her causing a ruckus at downtown bistros, flea markets or in her own backyard.

To my family for all your love and support; without you I would be out on the street begging for money.

Chapter 1

Olena Petrovich had had close to three hundred years to perfect sin to an art form. In the past, she'd used her vampiric charms to get whatever she wanted in life—money, sex, power. It helped, she supposed, that she was curvy and possessed a mouth some men had said was made for sin. But it had always proven to be too easy.

She didn't want easy any longer. She liked working for the things she received. Like this case.

This was Olena's first time as lead investigator and she was excited about it. She didn't want to make one mistake. It wasn't often that Inspector Gabriel Bellmonte let go of the reins. But he had for her. Or it could've been because she had begged him for the past three months.

The crime scene at the National Bank of Nouveau Monde wasn't typical for a bank robbery. Usually the robbers took the money, but instead these guys—four armed, masked men—had herded everyone in the bank into the vault, then blasted apart the safety-deposit boxes.

Olena and her team wouldn't be able to get a clear view of the situation until they'd pieced together all the boxes that had been destroyed. And by the looks of the mess, that was going to take considerable time.

The odor of smoke still hung oppressively in the air as Olena eyed the wall of boxes, taking in the destruction. Charred residue marred an array of the shiny metal squares in a circular pattern. The explosion had caused a lot of damage.

"I wonder what they were looking for." She glanced over her shoulder at her investigative partner, Sophie St. Clair, who was busy taking pictures of the metal and plastic shrapnel scattered all over the black-and-white-tiled floor.

"I guess someone must've lost his key." After

snapping her last photo, Sophie stood beside Olena and surveyed the destroyed wall. "Kellen called. He said he'd be on scene in about fifteen minutes," Sophie informed her.

Olena nodded. "Good. He can figure out this blast pattern on the remaining safety-deposit boxes."

Kellen, a recent addition to their crime-scene team, was a damn good ballistics expert. He had come from America to France for treatment for a rare blood disease and had ended up completely cured, with a new job on the team and an engagement to Sophie.

Fate had a grand sense of humor.

"What did the bank manager have to say?"

"He said that around nine-thirty, about the time that they open for business, four men with black ski masks burst into the bank, waving guns around, and told everyone to get facedown on the floor."

"Could he tell if they were vamps or lycans or anything?"

"No. He said he couldn't really get a bead on any of them." Olena frowned. "But he did say one of them smelled like menthol."

"The manager's a lycan?"

Olena nodded.

Sophie shrugged. "Maybe that guy had a cold and he's been using cold medicines."

"Yeah, that could be it."

"I have my moments." Sophie smiled.

"Once everyone was on the floor, one of the gunmen demanded that the manager open the vault and another two herded all the employees and patrons into it. The same one took the keys from the manager and shut the vault with everyone inside."

"So nobody saw anything after that?"

"No." Olena flipped her notebook open and read from her notes. "But three of the ten people in the vault said they heard an explosion at around ten-thirty."

Sophie glanced at her watch. "Let's see. It's one now, so two and a half hours. Not bad to be on scene already."

"A regular bank patron named Madame Fonteneau called 911 when she couldn't get into the bank at eleven-thirty." Olena smiled. "Whoever cased the bank didn't count on Mrs. Fonteneau's fortitude to cash her monthly social-security check."

"Did she see anything?"

Olena shook her head. "No. Unfortunately, she was so upset about not cashing her check that she cried through most of the interview." She flipped her notepad closed and slid it into the inner pocket of her blue nylon jacket, the standard coat for all crime-scene technicians.

A young police constable stuck his head into the room. "Here are all the tapes from the security cameras." He came in holding five tapes and handed them over to her.

"Thanks." She smiled at him.

He blushed and continued to gape at her.

She glanced around. "Is there something else, Officer…?"

"Anderson," he supplied. "Ah, yeah, sorry. There's a guy up front who asked to see whoever was in charge of the scene."

"Who is he?"

"I don't know, ma'am. My superior officer just told me to deliver the tapes and to escort you to the lobby of the bank."

Olena glanced at Sophie, who shrugged her shoulders. "Beats me. Could be from the mayor's office. This is the biggest and most prestigious bank in Nouveau Monde. I bet a lot of bigwigs bank here, and they're all worried about their money."

"I hope not. I hate bureaucrats. There's nothing more boring than someone with a political agenda."

Before following the officer out of the room, Olena bagged and tagged the security footage and placed it into her crime-scene collection suitcase.

As she walked behind Officer Anderson, he kept glancing at her over his shoulder with a goofy grin on his boyish face. Olena sighed inwardly. He couldn't have been more than twenty-three. A lycan, she had no doubt. A vampire wouldn't have been so eager to please her. He would've had enough years of experience that a mere innocent smile from an attractive woman wouldn't have sent him into a tizzy. Where were they getting these whelps? The puppy pound?

There was a lot of commotion in the lobby as Olena and the young officer approached. The bank manager looked as if he was arguing with another officer, frantically gesticulating.

The bank patrons who had been locked in the vault were still being interviewed. But standing out from all the commotion in the middle of the lobby, looking commanding but at ease, was a tall, ruggedly gorgeous man in an expensive-looking tailored suit.

Olena wasn't easily impressed. Having lived so long in many different countries, she'd come across her fair share of attractive men. Libertines, princes and lords, all with power, prestige and perfectly formed butts. But this man stood out from them all.

She thought it was because he didn't appear to be posturing for anyone or anything. He just was.

She wondered who he was. A high-powered investor inquiring about his holdings at the bank, or maybe the owner of one of the safety-deposit boxes, curious as to what had been stolen.

When the officer led her right to him, her heart picked up a few beats. And butterflies took flight in her stomach when his piercing gaze met hers and studied her with a clinical eye.

She was impressed. Most men started their study of her from the toes up, stopping periodically on her long legs and ample chest. His gaze never left her face.

Officer Anderson motioned toward the gentleman, then proceeded to move in another direction, his task complete.

"Are you in charge of this crime scene?" He had a deep voice and an accent. British, she thought, maybe Welsh. And he was definitely human.

"Yes. Olena Petrovich, NMPD crime-scene division." She offered her hand. "And you are?"

As he took her hand in a quick, firm shake, he flipped open a badge wallet. "Inspector Cale Braxton, Interpol." He shut the leather folder and slid it into his front pants pocket.

"Interpol? That's a first." She smiled, but he remained stoic.

"I've already spoken with Superintendent Jakob Weiss, and he assured me that there wouldn't be a problem."

"A problem with what? You have not even told me why you're here."

"This robbery. I'll be heading up the investigation."

Olena's stomach flipped over. It felt like the floor had just dropped out from beneath her feet. She hadn't worked this hard for this long to have her case yanked out from under her, not by anyone—even if he was a tall, light-brown-haired, ocean-blue-eyed, sexy man with a rugged jawline and full lips that looked as soft as satin.

"Why would Interpol get involved in a simple robbery case?"

"I'm sorry, but that information is above your pay grade." He stepped around her as if she were nothing. "Now, if you could lead me to the actual crime scene."

Olena looked him up and down, her first impression of him slowly starting to shift. She liked confidence in a man, even sought it out, but arrogance? That was one thing she could never stomach.

And this man had it in spades.

Instead of leading him anywhere, Olena dug into her jacket pocket, pulled out her cell phone and called Gabriel. She kept Cale's gaze as she dialed. He wasn't going to intimidate her. No one intimidated her. She'd been part of Marie Antoinette's court in France, for Pete's sake. One sexy British agent wasn't going to get under her skin.

He answered on the first shrill ring. "Inspector Bellmonte."

"Why is there a human from Interpol demanding to be on my crime scene?"

"He got there fast."

"I take it you know about this."

"Yes, but just barely. The call came in from the superintendent about five minutes ago. I was about to call you and give you a heads-up."

She turned away from Cale's gaze, not wanting

him to see the anger and disappointment on her face. She wasn't a woman who liked to be read easily. Her emotions were her own, and she didn't like anyone having an insight into them.

"I'm sorry, Olena. I know how much you wanted to lead this one. But I have strict orders from the superintendent to grant the agent anything he needs on this case. Interpol is running the show on this one."

"Fine. I'll try to be nice to Agent Braxton."

Cale cleared this throat at that, and she swung around to look at him. His lips twitched, and she could tell he was fighting a smile.

"Olena." She could hear the warning in Gabriel's voice. "Your nice and other people's nice are two entirely different things."

She smiled at that. Gabriel knew her too well.

"Be gentle with him. He's only human, after all. We don't want to send a broken agent back to Interpol. That's one kind of trouble this community doesn't need."

"I'll try, but I can't promise you anything." As she flipped her phone closed, she ran the tip of her tongue over her fangs. Cale watched the motion with interest. She smiled at his reaction.

No, she couldn't promise Gabriel anything. She

wasn't very good at playing nice, especially with men who thought they were superior. Agent Braxton needed to be knocked down a few notches, and she was just the vampiress for the job.

Chapter 2

Cale tried to keep his face stoic as he watched the vampiress run the tip of her tongue over her distended fangs. It proved difficult. She was unearthly beautiful and sexy. An exotic-looking goddess with a full, sensuous mouth and rich sable-colored hair—which she likely used to her advantage. Especially in situations like this one. But he wasn't going to let her play him.

He'd been played before by the same type of bewitching creature and lost a hell of a lot more than just the game. He wasn't about to let that happen again. No matter how tempted he was.

"The crime scene is where?" he asked again, surveying the main bank foyer.

Olena looked at him for a long moment with her luminous green eyes, then without a word turned on her heel and marched back toward the hallway from which she'd originally appeared. He followed her down the long corridor. He was loath to admit it, but he watched every sway of her derriere as she walked in front of him. She was wearing simple gray trousers, but even their plainness couldn't disguise the fact that the vampiress had amazing curves.

She glanced over her shoulder and caught him looking at her. The smile that came to her lips was one of triumph. He was going to have to be extra careful around her and guard his thoughts like Fort Knox. The woman was potent, and she obviously knew it.

Stopping at the end of the hallway, she gestured to the room with the bars. "We're in here."

With a polite nod in her direction, Cale passed by her, careful not to catch a whiff of her perfume. He'd always been attracted to a woman's smell. It was something that remained with him long after meeting the woman.

Unfortunately, he picked up her tantalizing scent. And it made the hairs on the back of his neck stir to attention. Damn, the woman was going to kill him, and he'd only just met her. If he had to work with her, it was going to be torture on his libido.

There was another CSI in the room when he entered. A redhead with a fierce gaze. And she pinned him with it the second he stepped onto the tiled floor.

"Qui est ceci?" the redhead asked of Olena.

"Interpol," she said as she walked into the room and stood beside the other investigator. "He's come to take over our crime scene."

He looked at the both of them giving him twin looks of distrust. A united front against his intrusion. But he had a job to do, and he'd do it whether they chose to cooperate or not.

"Look, Ms. Petrovich, I'm sorry if you think I'm stepping on your toes, but there is more at stake here than your ego."

Her eyebrows rose at that, and she glanced at her colleague, then back at him. He hadn't meant to insult her or get her back up, but it looked as if he'd managed to do both. He just wanted to do what he needed to do, then move on. The less time in the vampiress's presence the better. Sweat was already starting to drip down his back. He was known for being one of the coolest men in the agency, like ice under pressure, but this woman was testing him far beyond anything he'd experienced before. She had some power.

"Well, Agent Braxton, I believe the only ego we have to worry about on this case is yours. There's hardly enough room in here for the four of us."

The redhead looked from Olena to him and back, then gathered her camera and shoved it into her crime-scene kit. "Ah, I'm going to go take a break and see if I can catch Kellen before he interrupts this, um, conversation." With a backward glance at Olena, she made her escape.

It was obvious the vampiress wasn't going to make this easy on him. She stared at him, venom in her eyes, her arms crossed over her chest. She struck quite a menacing figure. Power radiated off her like a sonic beacon. Most humans would be cowering by now. But he wasn't like most humans. He'd been trained to work with Otherworlders. Trained in ways to combat their supernatural powers. He'd tangled with a lot of powerful folks both in and outside the Otherworld communities.

He'd battled with terrorists and evil men bent on destroying the world. He could handle this one woman.

He hoped.

"Could you turn down the power, Ms. Petrovich? I hardly think it's necessary, considering we're on the same side."

Her eyebrow rose again. "Are we really?" She gave him a slow, sly smile. The potency of it punched him in the gut. "I'll tell you what. When you show me some respect, I'll reciprocate." Her Russian accent thickened as she spoke.

Sighing, he pinched the bridge of his nose between thumb and forefinger. His head was starting to throb. As were other parts of his anatomy. "Let's start over, okay?"

She regarded him expectantly but made no move to concede to him.

"Interpol would like to help in this case. I can't tell you right now why that is, but if you could bring me up to speed on the particulars, I may be able to divulge certain aspects that we are interested in."

"Hmm, that looked like it hurt." Olena let her arms fall to her sides, and her smile became more genuine.

"It did, a little."

"Now we can get down to business." She approached him with a swagger in her step and filled him in on the details. "As far as anyone can tell, they only took whatever was in those boxes. Henri, the bank manager, will do a thorough inventory of their money reserves, but so far that doesn't look like what they were interested in."

"Do you have a register of who owned the boxes?"

"Not yet. But Henri assures me he will get me one as soon as possible."

"I'm sure with a little pressure we can make it even sooner than that." He walked around the vault, taking in the damage. They were smart, these thieves. They knew exactly what they were doing and exactly where to place their explosive charges. They weren't amateurs.

"Do you know what they were looking for?" Olena asked from beside him.

"Maybe."

"You know but won't tell me, or you don't know quite yet? Or is it all above my pay grade?"

Cale glanced at her. She was eyeing him with one elegant eyebrow arched. Most women couldn't pull off a look like that, but Olena did it with style. "It's not important right now. Right now, we need to establish a timeline, and we need a list of names."

"The timeline's been established."

"Okay, then maybe you could go talk to Henri again about those names."

The temperature in the room dropped by at least six degrees. He shivered inside his suit jacket. The look Olena gave him was one of bitter fury. If he'd been another man, he might've been afraid. But he'd been around a lot of tough people in his life, so one angry vampiress didn't scare him too much. He knew she could end his life in a matter of seconds, but he also knew she wouldn't. She was a professional. He could tell that about her the moment he met her gaze in the bank lobby.

"Do you always get your way, Agent Braxton?"

"Yes."

"Well, so do I." Her eyes flashed green fire at him. "You're what, thirty-four? I've had at least two hundred and forty more years of practice at it than you. So who do you think is going to win this battle in the end?" With that, she walked out of the room.

He watched her leave, struck by the intensity

of her power. He'd never met a vampire that old before. He should've known she possessed that much force. He'd been trained to figure out the ages of vampires by the amount of sway they had on him and others. Olena just about had him on his knees. It probably irked her to no end that he could control his reactions to her as much as he did. He was only human, after all. That was probably what angered her the most.

Shaking his head to clear her from his mind, Cale glanced down at the metal shrapnel on the tiled floor. Now that he was alone, it was time he got to work. This was something he had to do without an audience. He wasn't ready quite yet to let others know what he could do.

Crouching, he reached for a piece of one of the safety-deposit boxes and carefully picked it up between two fingers. He closed his eyes and let his mind go.

Chapter 3

Trying to control her anger, Olena caught up with Sophie and Kellen in the bank foyer. They were both drinking coffee. She could use some caffeine herself right about now.

As she neared, Sophie handed her the third cup, which had been waiting for her on the marble table in the foyer. "That bad?"

Olena took the offered drink, sipped it and sighed. Sophie knew her well. "Do you think Interpol would really look for an agent if he just vanished into thin air?"

"I know some killer places to hide a body. No

one would ever find him," Kellen said after taking a sip of his coffee.

Sophie gave her fiancé a skeptical look. "You'd better be kidding."

"Of course I am." He hugged the spitfire lycan to him but winked at Olena over the top of Sophie's head.

"I saw that."

"Saw what?"

Olena left the newly engaged, squabbling lovers and wandered off to find the bank manager. She could at least accomplish something on this case. If she was being forced to work with Agent Braxton, at least she could uncover a piece of evidence before he did. She hated that he made her feel competitive. She didn't usually act that way on a case. No matter who cracked what, the crime-scene investigation team was always the one to benefit. No one member stood out among the others.

But Cale wasn't part of her team.

Henri, the bank manager, was busy at his desk answering the phone. When he saw Olena approach, his face brightened. He hung up the phone as she stepped into his office.

"I was just going to come find you." He grabbed

a piece of paper off his desk. "I have that list for you."

Olena went to take the paper, but at the last second she sensed movement behind her. She turned to find Cale standing at her left shoulder, reaching for the list just as she had been.

He grasped it between his fingers. "I'll take that, thank you."

"What do you think you're doing?" she asked.

"My job." He folded the piece of paper and slid it into the inside pocket of his suit jacket.

She was speechless. She'd never met a more infuriating male, human or otherwise, in her whole life, and she'd had a lot of years and men to choose from. Even Rasputin had more manners than Agent Cale Braxton.

"We're done here." He turned and walked out of Henri's office.

Olena followed behind, her hands fisted at her sides. She had to bite down on her tongue to stop herself from calling him some choice names.

"We are certainly not done here. The scene still needs to be processed, the evidence from the explosion collected and transported to the lab."

"It's being done as we speak." He stopped at

the front doors of the bank and glanced back at her. "I already sent your team in to finish up."

"You ordered my team?" She couldn't stop the quiver in her voice. "You?" She pointed at him, fighting the urge to actually stab him in the chest with her nail.

"There is your kit." He nodded toward the corner of the foyer. "Now you and I can go back to NMPD headquarters and get to work on this list." He reached into his suit jacket, pulled out a pair of black sunglasses and slid them on. "Do you have a car?" He pushed through the revolving glass door.

After quickly grabbing her crime-scene kit, Olena followed him out, fuming and at a loss for words. She had a couple of options, she figured. Suck it up and play nice with the human, or switch the game to her rules.

"I have a car." She pointed to the black sedan parked half a block down. "Over there."

He looked at her sideways, then nodded.

She led him to the car. Taking the keys out of her jacket, she unlocked the driver's door and the trunk with the remote. "I'll just put this in the car and we can be off."

Olena went around back, dropped her kit in, slammed the trunk closed, then opened her door.

She slid into the driver's seat and put the key into the ignition. Cale stood on the curb waiting for her to unlock the passenger door, fiddling with what looked like a BlackBerry.

Time to change the rules.

She opened the passenger window. He glanced down at her through the open window, one eyebrow raised in question.

"Hey, Braxton." She smiled sweetly at him. "I'll see you at the lab. If you can find your way there."

With that, she put the car in drive and sped away from the curb. Cale didn't even have a chance to reach for the door.

It was a juvenile thing to do, but as she watched his stunned reaction, then his slow, sexy grin in the rearview mirror, she knew it was worth it. Smiling to herself, she slid in a Paramour CD and put on her black-tinted sunglasses. It was turning out to be a perfectly beautiful, sunny day.

Chapter 4

It took Cale forty extra minutes to secure a ride to NMPD headquarters after the vampiress left him stranded on the curb. She'd taken him by surprise when she'd driven off like that. He wasn't usually surprised by people, having trained extensively in human behavior. But Olena Petrovich wasn't in any way human. Again, he had to remind himself to be ready for anything around the vampiress. She was, to say the least, unpredictable.

And he had to admit that intrigued him about her. Probably more than it should have. He'd known vampires before, interacted with them, worked with them, and he'd found most to be very ingrained in their ways, not open to change. He found that to be a contradiction, since many of them had seen centuries of change over their long lives. On the other hand, maybe that was why most held on to their old ways so tightly.

He didn't sense that with Olena.

When he arrived at the NMPD headquarters, he was impressed with the facility. It was a bright, open building, aesthetically pleasing, and by the looks of the equipment he'd seen in some of the rooms as he walked down the hallway to the lab, very well-equipped with up-to-date technology. He was pleased about that, since he'd had some concerns about working this case outside of Interpol offices.

But add in one distracting vampiress and he still had some doubts.

Another few strides down the hall and he found what he'd been looking for. He gave a few quick raps on the door, then entered Inspector Gabriel Bellmonte's office.

The man, a lycan, Cale had heard, was behind his desk. He glanced up as Cale walked into the room, seemingly not surprised at all by his appearance. "Agent Braxton, I presume."

Cale nodded. "Yes. How did you know?"

Gabriel tapped his nose. "I could smell you coming down the hall." Leaning forward, he placed his elbows on his desk and motioned Cale toward a chair. "Plus I saw Olena earlier, and she informed me that you'd be on your way here."

"Yes. It seems your investigator has forgotten the meaning of cooperation," Cale said as he slid into the offered seat.

The inspector smiled. "Oh, she knows what it means, Agent Braxton."

Cale kept the lycan's gaze. It was fierce, and a lesser man might have bent to the predator's will. But Cale wasn't a lesser man. He'd dealt with lycans on several occasions. He liked most that he met. He considered them a stout and loyal species, and Gabriel was no different. Cale suspected he'd fight to the death for one of his own—and for the investigators on his team, regardless of whether they were lycan. That obviously included Olena. Cale would get no help from him in dealing with the vampiress.

After a few more seconds, letting the inspector know that he wasn't afraid of him, Cale lowered his gaze. He gave the encounter up to Gabriel. He was in his territory, so it was only wise that Cale show deference to the man in charge.

"Do you have a room I could use to set up a base for this investigation?"

"Of course." Gabriel stood and came around the desk.

Cale followed the lycan out of the office and down the hallway. When they reached another closed door, the inspector opened it and gestured for Cale to go through.

"I was wondering when you'd get here." Olena sat in a chair behind one of the three computers in the room, never taking her eyes off the screen as she spoke.

"I'll let you two get reacquainted," Gabriel said. "I'll go see if Kellen and Sophie are back with the evidence from the scene." He shut the door behind him.

Cale moved to stand behind Olena. He noticed she was doing a name search in a database. "What are you looking for?" He reached into his suit pocket and slid out the paper the bank manager had given him.

"I'm running the names from Henri's list in a bunch of different databases to see if anything comes up." She glanced back at him and gave him that seductive grin of hers. "I had Henri fax me a copy of the list. I don't like to be idle."

He slid the list back into his pocket. "Clever."

"I know." Reaching with her long leg, she hooked the chair at the next computer station and rolled it closer to her. She patted the cushion. "Here. Why don't you take off that stuffy suit jacket, loosen your tie and have a seat. This may take a while to run through."

The way she was looking at him made him want to do more than take off his suit jacket and sit beside her. Carnal thoughts raced through his mind like quicksilver. They came so quick, so fierce that he had trouble putting together a coherent sentence. He'd never met a vampire who possessed that much seductive power. The muscles in his legs clenched as he forced them to stay put, a safe distance from Olena where he could not react to his inner desires.

But as quickly as she'd given him that look, it disappeared when she gave her attention back to the computer screen. Once more he could breathe easily and not think about the twenty different ways he could take her right here in this room.

Rolling his neck to loosen the tension he felt there, he shucked off his jacket, hung it up on the back of the chair and sat down, careful not to brush up against Olena.

She glanced at him sideways. "Is there something wrong? You seem really tense."

"I'm sure you know why."

"No, I'm sorry. I don't think I know what you're talking about." She said the words with innocence, but he caught the flare of her eyebrow and the coy lift of her mouth when she turned her head.

Before he could respond, something popped up on the computer screen.

"We got a hit." Olena typed in a command and the full-screen photo and information appeared on the screen. "Looks like one of our safety-deposit box owners has a criminal record."

Sliding closer to the computer, Cale read the information on the screen. *Marie Morgan, age 45, lycan, arrested and convicted of assault causing bodily harm.* The facts were interesting, but from the information swirling in his head, he knew Ms. Morgan wasn't right.

He shook his head. "She's not the person we're looking for."

Olena glanced at him. "How do you know?"

"I just do. She doesn't fit the profile."

"What profile? I didn't know there was one."

He didn't answer her, but rolled back in his chair, painfully aware of how close he'd been to her. Her scent tickled his nose.

"What is it that you're not telling me?" After a moment, she put up her hand. "Forget it. I know what it is you're not telling me. Everything." She pushed away from the computer desk and strode to the door.

Before she could open it, he asked, "Where are you going?"

"To work on another case," she replied without turning around. "It's obvious you don't need me on this. I'm sure you can manage on your own, Agent Braxton."

Running a hand over his jaw, he sighed. The woman knew exactly what buttons to push. "The item that was stolen from the bank is a matter of international security. We have reason to believe that the people responsible for the theft may have terrorist connections."

Olena turned around and walked back to the desk. She sat down. "Can you tell me what exactly we're supposed to be looking for?"

"No. In truth, we're not completely sure, but we have our suspicions. And those will remain top secret."

"So, we don't know what was in thc box, to whom the box belongs or who robbed it."

"That pretty much sums it up."

She eyed him carefully. He had the sense that she was probing him, could see right through him to the other side. After another second she grinned. "You're here on your own, aren't you?"

That statement took him aback. "I'm not sure I get what you mean."

"I bet if I called the main Interpol office they wouldn't have any idea that you're here and working on this case."

"I'm not sure why you would think that."

"Because I know a rogue when I see one."

He kept her gaze. It was fierce, but there was something else there behind the crystalline green depths. A sense of recognition, a kinship. He liked that. But he still wasn't sure what to divulge to her and what to keep to himself. He trusted her to a point. But trust had gotten him into loads of trouble.

"I'm here on my own, yes. When I heard about the robbery, I had a hunch about it, and I informed my superiors that I was going to check it out. They trust my hunches, so they allowed me to come here."

She cocked her head and scrutinized him even more. Sweat trickled down his back from her examination. She would make an incredible inquisitor. Maybe he could set her up with a job at the agency.

"You *heard* about the robbery?"

He nodded, but his tie seemed to be choking him.

"You were in the bank only hours after it happened. I'd just heard about it and I was only a half hour from the site. You would have had to have flown in from somewhere." She frowned. "That's pretty quick. Or maybe you fly as fast as Superman."

"Some things are going to remain classified, Olena. That would be one of them."

She pursed her full mouth as if considering the statement. "I'll keep your secrets, but only because I like the way you say my name."

Finally, she turned toward the computer and set her long, elegant fingers on the keyboard. "So, a female lycan isn't what we're looking for."

He rolled his chair a little closer to her. "Definitely male. But I'm not sure what species. Vampire, I think."

"Well, that narrows it down." She typed in a

few more commands, and the screen filled with information. Two names popped up. But before she could do anything further, her cell phone vibrated against the desk.

She picked it up. "Petrovich." After a few moments, she turned and smiled at Cale. Every time she did that, his heart rate accelerated. He was going to have to work on controlling that. Because he was certain that Olena could hear it.

"Thanks, Kellen. That was quick work." She snapped the phone closed. "Box one hundred and thirty-six."

Cale picked up the list of box owners on the desk and scanned the contents. His eyes rested on the name beside box number one hundred and thirty-six. "Luc Dubois."

Olena pointed at the ID photo of a middle-aged man with long black hair on the computer screen. "And we have a winner."

Chapter 5

With Gabriel's blessing, Olena drove herself and Cale out to Luc Dubois's place of residence. They didn't have a warrant, but they hoped he'd speak to them regardless. Olena figured he'd be anxious to get back whatever it was that had been stolen. Unless, of course, that item was of a questionable nature—which she assumed it was, or the sexy British agent wouldn't be in her city.

She was a bit more relaxed around Cale now that he'd confessed the agency wasn't behind him. She liked that he was out on his own working this case, that he followed his instincts. Another man may not have been so courageous as to step out of the ranks to go it alone.

She also sensed there was something he was keeping hidden. Not about the case, but about himself. She didn't believe for one second that he'd come to Nouveau Monde after the explosion. It was physically impossible. Cale had been on his way there before the explosion even occurred, and she really wanted to know why. But she suspected he wasn't going to tell her. Not easily, anyway.

She had her ways, though. It would be just a matter of time before he was confessing all his secrets to her.

She smiled, thinking about all the delicious ways she could torture the information out of him.

"What's funny?"

She glanced at him, careful not to rake her gaze over his body and give away all her thoughts. "Nothing of consequence."

"Somehow I don't believe that. I think everything you do is of significance. Especially to those around you."

"Hmm, I'm not quite sure how to take that. You're either insulting me or complimenting me."

"It wasn't an insult." He turned his head to look out the window.

Olena put her attention back onto the road. But she had to admit she really liked looking at Cale. He was delectably put together. His strong jaw, with just the hint of stubble, begged her to stroke a finger or run her tongue over it. His high cheekbones seemed cut from stone, and his straight nose reminded her of a royal bloodline. She would know, as she'd been around her fair share of kings, princes and lords in several different countries and centuries.

She wondered not for the first time what he'd look like underneath the crisp press of his suit and white shirt. He'd taken off the jacket at least, but had yet to loosen his tie. She hoped he'd let her do that for him. There was nothing more erotic than undressing a sharply dressed man. Shedding the stiff exterior to discover the wild, untamed man beneath.

A shiver rushed through her just thinking about it. Cale must have sensed it, because he looked at her with that sexy lift of his eyebrow.

"Are you cold?"

"Not at all." She grinned at him.

He turned to look out the window again, likely trying to avoid her predatory gaze.

He thought she was using her powers against

him. Olena wondered what he'd do if he knew she hadn't spiked her power levels once since meeting him. Whatever was zipping between them was one hundred percent natural.

It would probably bring him no relief to know that it surprised her as well.

Olena pulled the vehicle up to the curb in front of a lavish home. Luc Dubois lived in a gated community usually reserved for the rich and famous. She didn't recognize his name offhand, so she didn't think he was a celebrity, and she knew almost all of the vampire elite in Nouveau Monde. This man was flying under her radar.

"What does this guy do for a living?" Cale asked.

"I'm not sure. The bank doesn't keep those types of records for safety-deposit boxes. Privacy issues."

Cale opened his door and slid out of the car. Olena followed suit and stood beside him on the walkway to the front door.

"Do you have a weapon?" he asked, taking in the layout of the house and street.

"I have plenty."

He looked at her. "Are you armed?"

Olena unzipped her nylon jacket and parted it

to the right to show him the gun on her hip. "Standard issue. Silver bullets. Although that wouldn't stop a vampire if he wanted to hurt someone."

"No, but it might make him think twice about it."

Olena patted him on the shoulder. "Don't worry, Cale. I'll protect you. I'm faster and meaner than most."

"I'll remember that."

"Please do." With that, she started up the walkway. She didn't wait to see if Cale followed. If he was up on his species, he'd know all about the politics that played out in the vampire society. During this meeting, Olena would be doing all the talking. Humans weren't high on most vampires' respect list. Except for blood donations and sex, humans weren't regarded much at all.

Olena didn't agree with the structure, though. She liked humans. Over the years, she'd had her fair share of human lovers, and loves. All of them were long dead now, to her regret, and it had been a while since her last human lover. Contrary to what most people thought, she didn't engage in a lot of casual sex. More often than not, she developed feelings. She was just really good at masking them as indifference and flamboyancy. In fact, though, she'd had her heart broken many times over watching the men she'd loved die.

She didn't have any plans on going through that again. Not even for a man as attractive as Cale. She'd flirt with him, toy with him to get what she wanted, but she refused to ever get involved. Her heart couldn't take it. She'd spent the past thirty years mending it, and she wasn't about to wreck any of that progress. No matter how much she wanted to peel away his serious layers and discover the passion inside. She sensed the man would be explosive if prodded just the right way. And she knew all the right ways to prod.

Standing on the doorstep, Olena waited until Cale was at her side before she rang the bell. She counted to three under her breath, then rang it again and added three sharp raps to the door. After a few moments, there was still no answer.

She put her ear to the door. She was no lycan, but her hearing was far superior to a human's. She didn't hear any movement inside, but she did hear the faint thumping of some type of dance or hip-hop music.

"Anything?"

"Music. Either someone's home, or they left their radio on somewhere in the house."

Cale cupped his hands against the window in the sidelight door and peered inside. He shook his head. "I don't see anything." He backed off the doorstep and headed around the side. "Let's check around back."

Getting around back proved to be difficult. A high wrought-iron fence with a locked gate bracketed the backyard.

Cale looked it over, then glanced at Olena. One eyebrow went up in a question. "Any ideas?"

"If I find a way in, I'll open the front door for you." She winked at him, then, backing up a few steps, ran forward and leaped into the air.

She soared over the fence, the heels of her shoes just brushing the tips of the iron spikes at the top of the fence. When she landed on the other side, she glanced over her shoulder at Cale.

He was shaking his head, but she caught the grin he was trying to quell.

"Wish you could do that, don't you?"

"Maybe." This time the smile came freely. And it was dazzling. A little quiver erupted in her belly. It had been a long time since she'd had that kind of reaction to anyone.

"I won't be long," she said as she made her way toward the pool area and sliding glass doors.

"Be careful," he called out after her.

She paused at that and looked back. He was watching her through the fence. She gave him a little wave and continued on. Why on earth would he be worried about her? She was the stronger one here. The one with the enhanced strength and durability. Must be a man thing.

Olena walked along the stone path through the yard, around the pool and up to the sliding glass doors. The blinds were open and she peered in. There was no sign of anyone in the house, at least not in the back part. Someone could've still been upstairs, or in the basement for that matter. She imagined Luc had a basement; most vampires with big homes did. It was usually the place where they slept and engaged in other activities if they were so inclined.

She rapped on the glass door, but there was no response. Taking out a latex glove from her coat pocket, she slid it on, then grasped the handle. Unlocked, the door slid open with no effort.

She poked her head in. "Hello? Monsieur Dubois? I'm from the crime-scene investigation team."

There was no response.

But Olena did pick up the strong smell of blood.

She slid the door all the way open, drew her weapon and stepped into the house. Now that she was inside, she could hear the music a little better. It was definitely hip-hop. She crept through the kitchen, down the hallway and to the large front foyer. So far, she hadn't seen any blood spots or bodies. She threw open the lock and opened the front door for Cale.

"I smell blood," she told him.

He came into the house and drew his own weapon. He looked around the front entrance, taking in everything and, by the way his nostrils flared, trying to smell the blood. "I didn't realize vampires had a heightened sense of smell."

"We don't for most things. But blood we can scent from a long distance."

"Makes sense." He looked past her from where she came. "Did you see anything?"

She shook her head. "I came through the kitchen. It's clean."

"Where's the music coming from?"

"The basement."

He nodded and motioned for her to continue.

Olena retraced her steps and went back toward the kitchen. There was a door along one wall and she suspected it led to the basement.

When she reached it, she glanced over her shoulder at Cale. He was poised behind her, his gun ready. She was impressed that he hadn't demanded to go first, like most men would have. But Cale seemed quite comfortable with Olena in the lead. Maybe he understood that he was human and much more vulnerable than she. It was nice to meet a man who understood the balance of nature.

"On three," she said to him. He nodded. Wrapping her hand around the doorknob, she whispered, "One, two, three." She turned the knob and swung open the door. Cale was there at the opening, his weapon pointed. But nothing jumped out at them.

Olena peered down the stairs. There were lights on, and the music was much louder.

"I'll go down first," she said. "Stay behind me. If anything should get by me, make sure you go for the head. A head shot will slow anything down."

"I'm fully aware of how to kill, Olena," he said. "I've had my fair share of run-ins with members of the Otherworld community."

"I'm just making sure. I really don't want to send your shredded body back to your bosses. I hate having to explain things like that."

"Thanks for your concern."

She smiled at him and started down the steps. As she moved she could feel him behind her. True to his word, he was pressed in close to her back. She liked that he was seeking protection from her. There was nothing more Olena liked than control.

When they reached the bottom of the stairs, the smell of blood intensified. From the way Cale's nose wrinkled, he could smell it as well. But so far they didn't see any crimson pools or a body.

The basement was obviously where Luc played. A billiards table and a dartboard were set up near what looked to be a fully stocked bar. A huge projection TV with surround sound took up one wall. Olena counted about ten speakers mounted nearby. The music was coming from a state-of-the-art high-tech sound system mounted on the wall, shelves of CDs surrounding it.

The walls and the floor were done in an old-world tavern style. Hardwood floors, wooden bar stools, wood paneling on the walls with what appeared to be oil lamps lighting the way. Olena liked it. It made her homesick for a few of her old haunts in London and Paris back in the early 1900s.

"Looks like he's a big entertainer," Cale said as he inspected the full bar. He motioned toward three half-full glasses on the counter. "And he had company."

Olena carefully made her way to another door in the corner. She didn't think it led to the bathroom. The scent of blood was strongest coming from underneath the door.

"I have a feeling he did some other types of entertaining as well."

Cale came over to her as she slowly opened the heavy wooden door. He produced a flashlight from one of his pockets and shone it into the dark room.

It was what Olena had suspected. Luc Dubois was one of those vampires who got off on the pain and suffering of others, or in some cases, their own.

As Cale swung the light around the room, they could plainly see the iron manacles fastened to the wall, a padded wooden horse in the middle of the room likely used for punishment, both sexual and otherwise, and the rack mounted on the wall with varying instruments of pain and pleasure.

What they didn't expect to see was a completely naked Luc Dubois—or what Olena thought was him—also fastened on the wall by several wooden stakes. Without his head.

Chapter 6

Cale cursed. He'd seen pictures of vampire-killing scenes but never been witness to one. It was disturbing on many levels.

He glanced at Olena and saw that she'd gone deathly still. He holstered his weapon then put his hand on her shoulder. "Are you okay?"

She nodded, but he could tell that she wasn't. Her body was vibrating, and her naturally pale skin had gone even paler. Wrapping his hand around her shoulder, he pulled her to him. She let him. He knew then that she must've been in shock, otherwise he was sure she would've pulled away from him, not wanting to appear weak.

He didn't think she could appear weak in any circumstances.

Cale wrapped his arms around her and steered her away from the open door. She held on to his shirt and nuzzled her face into his shoulder. Acting on instinct, he ran a hand down over her hair. It was silky smooth under his palm, and he had to fight the urge to bury his fingers in it.

"Just give me a minute," she said, still clutching his shirt. "I'll be fine."

"Okay." Was it wrong of him to want her to take her time? To want her to need to hang onto him for support, for comfort? She felt so right in his arms. He liked the way they fit together, like interlocking puzzle pieces.

After a few more moments, she breathed deeply, then uncurled her fingers from his shirt and took a distancing step back. She brushed the front of her jacket, as if to sweep away the moment.

"It's been a while since I've seen a vampire execution." She didn't make eye contact with Cale as she spoke, but looked toward the open door.

"Is that what this is?"

She nodded. "Someone wanted to make an example of him. It's a message."

"To whom?"

She shook her head. "Someone who knows Luc Dubois. A business partner maybe, or a relative." Olena took out her cell phone. "I'd better call this in and get the team down here."

"While you do that, I'm going to go in and look around. See if I can find his head."

She nodded, then walked away from the room to call Inspector Bellmonte. He was glad for the reprieve, as it would afford him the privacy to do what he needed to do.

He went into the room and scanned the walls for a light switch. He found only five oil lamps along the wall. Without matches, he'd have to make do with the flashlight.

Mindful of where he was stepping, Cale neared the impaled body. As if an insect on display, five wooden stakes pinned the victim to the wall, one each in his arms and legs and one through his heart. The assailant or assailants had to have been very strong to be able to hold a vampire still enough to impale him with stakes into wallboard. That took a lot of power and finesse. Cale's money was on another vampire, or two.

He peered at the stakes. There was nothing remarkable about them. Just the standard wooden stake, oak most likely. He imagined a person could pick them up anywhere, on eBay even, or they could be homemade. Either way, they'd be virtually untraceable—to modern-day investigative techniques. He had something else in mind.

Glancing at the doorway to make sure he was alone, Cale rubbed his fingers together on his right hand. Carefully, he reached for the stake impaling the body through the heart. He touched the end of the wood. Nothing hit him immediately, so he moved his fingers down over the slope of the stake, searching for that thin thread that would connect him.

After another few seconds of searching, he found what he was looking for. Like a shock of adrenaline, heat surged through his fingers and up his arm. Closing his eyes, he saw ragged snippets of images coming at him at a rapid-fire pace.

A room. Small, cramped and dirty. Two men, with vague faces that he couldn't discern, talking. But Cale couldn't hear the words. Another scene flashed by. A van. Again something old and dirty. Two different men. Then Luc Dubois's front door. It opened, and a man Cale assumed to be Luc smiled and let the men in. After that, the images flashed by too fast, too blurred by the speed. But Cale saw blood, lots and lots of blood. And the last image, which seemed to last longer than the others, was the face of a young woman, a teenager perhaps, with piercing blue eyes. Then everything went blank.

He blinked open his eyes as he dropped his hand from the stake. His fingers tingled from the energy that had flowed out of it and into him. The feeling always lasted for a few hours afterward. But he figured it was worth it, considering the information he was usually able to glean. This time it hadn't been so easy. Violence like this usually left a bad essence. And he unfortunately could feel it through his thoughts.

"You're a touch telepath."

Startled, Cale turned toward the door. Olena stood in the doorway, watching him. He couldn't read the look on her face, but it definitely wasn't surprise he was seeing.

He clenched his hand tight, trying to push the tingling sensation away, but it was as stubborn as he was. He moved toward her.

"Why didn't you say anything?" she asked.

"I don't like to advertise it."

"Why?"

He didn't meet her gaze. He didn't want her to know that he wasn't proud of his power. When he was younger it had been a nuisance. Now it was just a tool for him to use on his job.

"Why do you think?"

"Because you don't want to be a freak. Because you were teased as a child, maybe even feared because of the things you could see."

He met her gaze then. She was perceptive. Unnervingly so. "I wasn't teased for long."

She shook her head. "No, I imagine after a while you probably beat the crap out of anyone who said anything to you."

He smiled then. "Yeah, that about sums it up."

"Does Interpol know about your gift?"

"My immediate boss, maybe a few other key players." He rubbed his hand on his pants. It still tingled. "That's why they indulge my 'feelings.'"

With narrowed eyes, she looked at him. "Can you read people?"

"No, just objects. People are much too complicated to get a bead on." He turned off his flashlight and slipped it into his jacket. She was still watching him with a wariness he hadn't seen from her before. "Are you worried that I've peeked into your head?"

"Not at all. With me, pretty much what you see is what you get."

He eyed her, likely lingering too long on her glorious mouth. "I highly doubt that."

She smiled then. "You know, Cale, you choose the most interesting times and places to flirt. That says a lot about you, don't you think?"

"I'm not flirting." He smoothed a hand down his tie. At least he didn't think he was deliberately flirting with her.

"Right, tell that to the ton of pheromones you're giving off." Before he could answer, she strolled back into the game room. "The team is on its way. I'm going to go to the car, get my kit and start dusting the scene."

Discreetly, Cale sniffed at himself. Was he really producing that much? Could she really smell it, or was she just yanking his chain? He was a sick bastard to be thinking about sex at a crime scene, but he had to admit that every time Olena was near him, carnal thoughts blasted his mind like dynamite. Unfortunately, his body was feeling the effects.

Chapter 7

They found Luc Dubois's head in the master bedroom, propped up on a pillow at the foot of his bed. Olena thought it was very *Godfather*-like. It reminded her of Mafia-style warfare. Vampire society was hierarchical, but she didn't think it functioned like the mob. It was based more in aristocracy, with lords and ladies and those who had money and power.

But power was power, no matter how one achieved it or wielded it.

And whoever had executed and decapitated

Luc Dubois possessed power. Or at the very least desired it greatly.

The team had processed the basement, bagging and tagging the three glasses, the body, and then the head after the coroner had come and done his thing. Olena had dusted for prints and found a lot of smudges on the pool cues, the pool balls and the equipment in the makeshift dungeon. It was obvious the victim did a lot of entertaining. Going through those prints was going to be like sifting through sugar for a grain of salt.

And once Gabriel had done some digging, they knew why the vampire had been so popular. Luc Dubois had been the owner and proprietor of several fashionable nightclubs around the city. Both mainstream human clubs and Otherworlder bars. One in particular stood out. Phantasia, a well-known magic sex club that had organized-crime ties.

When Gabriel had mentioned it to Cale, the agent's eyes had lit up. Gabriel had agreed that Olena would head over there with Cale to interview the regulars just as soon as the crime scene was finished and Phantasia was in full swing. Olena glanced at her watch. It was only around nine at night, still too early to go to the club.

And by the looks of Cale, discreetly yawning behind his hand, he needed a couple of hours' rest before they continued.

Clicking her kit shut, she walked to where he leaned against the wall and watched as the team finished up their work. "Looks like you could use some rest."

"I'm fine. I can go forty-eight hours if need be."

"Well, this isn't a need be situation." She made a point of looking at her watch again. "We have a good five hours before the club is in full swing. I could take you to your hotel and you could catch a couple of hours of sleep."

"What about you?"

She smiled. "I'm a night owl."

"Okay. I could stand to change my shirt, anyway. And I'd like to read up on these organized-crime links to the victim."

She left her kit with Gabriel and let him know that she was taking Cale to his hotel and then would pick him up again to go down to the club. The inspector just nodded and gave her one of his good-luck pats on the back.

The drive to Cale's downtown hotel was quiet. Cale was busy on his BlackBerry as Olena drove.

She didn't want to talk, anyway. After seeing a decapitated body and then finding the head propped up like a door prize, what did someone talk about?

Olena had seen vampires executed before. One didn't live as long as she had and not see things like that. But the last execution had been over sixty years ago. She had hoped the world had moved past that kind of barbaric behavior. Obviously, that was a wishful fantasy.

She had reacted strongly to the scene. It had proved a moment of weakness. And in that weakness she had allowed Cale to comfort her. He had surprised her by the gentleness of his embrace and the intimate way he'd stroked her hair. The moment had obviously weakened him as well. He didn't strike her as the kind of man to crumble under pressure or soften with sympathy. But he had. With her. She could still remember the way his heart had picked up a beat when he held her close, and the enticing scent of his cologne. It had sent a signal straight to the heart of her. Her belly had tightened and she'd been close to quivering in his arms.

She was definitely not a woman who quivered easily. And not when sex wasn't involved. Cale was starting to seep into her psyche. And she didn't like that much. She could feel herself losing her footing. Soon, if she didn't check herself, she'd be falling right into his waiting arms.

When she pulled up to the hotel, she had every intention of just dropping him off and going on her way. But when she parked, he looked at her with something akin to need in his eyes. Or maybe it was just desire. And then, on the pretense of food and conversation, he invited her to his room.

It was very difficult for a vampiress to say no to an invitation.

So she parked the car and followed him up to his room. She told herself that she was indeed hungry and that she couldn't do the case any good if she was light-headed from not eating. Vampires had quick metabolisms and needed to refuel constantly with either food or blood or both.

As they walked down the corridor toward his fifth-floor room, Olena stopped at one of the vending machines. She popped in the change and pressed the button for AB positive. It was her favorite type. When she reached down to snatch the bottle from the bin, she caught Cale's expression.

She arched one brow in question as she unscrewed the cap on the bottle. "You don't mind, do you? I'm parched."

He shook his head, but as she started to drink, his face visibly paled. Interesting. She hadn't thought he had any fear of Otherworlders when she first met him. He'd been confident, cocky even, and totally unafraid of their special differences. But there was something there. Fear possibly, but likely something else.

They continued to walk as she drank. When they reached his hotel room door, she finished the last of the blood, wiped her mouth with the back of her hand and dropped the bottle into the recycle bin along one wall. Nouveau Monde was a very green city.

Cale slid the key card into the slot and opened the door. Olena followed him in and shut the door behind her. He tossed his suit jacket onto the sofa in the living area as he walked toward the bedroom door.

"I'm going to change. Make yourself comfortable."

"Are you hungry? I could call room service."

"Sure," he said from the bedroom.

Olena picked up the phone, then set it down

again. She glanced toward the partially open bedroom door, then down to the floor. Her heart rate had picked up a little. Cale's scent was a lot more intense and concentrated in the room. She had to make a conscious effort not to inhale it and sigh from its full, rich aroma.

Clenching her hands into fists, she did a circuit around the room, trying hard not to think about him naked as he changed his clothes. But she couldn't help the images that popped into her mind. She imagined the width of his broad shoulders and the slope of his chest to his hard, flat stomach. She had no doubt that he'd have ripples of muscle all the way down to the waistband of his pants. She wondered if there would be a line of hair to follow or if he was smooth all over.

She swallowed the saliva pooling in her mouth and did another quick trip around the room. But it didn't help. She ended up at the bedroom door. She pushed it open and walked in.

Cale was standing near the bed with his back to the door, shirtless. He'd been reaching for another shirt that was laid out on the bed when she entered. He turned around, his face dark with either anger or desire. She couldn't tell which. It didn't matter. She'd take either.

"I was going to ask you what you wanted to eat." She took a step closer. "But then I realized I didn't really care."

"Olena…"

"Yeah, I know. This is a bad idea. And I told myself I didn't really want you, that having you would be a huge mistake. But I don't really care about that, either. Not right now."

He had yet to cover himself. And she'd been right about his shoulders and his hard, rippling stomach. His chest was smooth except for a small patch of brown hair around his navel. Olena wanted to run her fingers through that hair as she lowered the zipper on his trousers.

"You've had a bit of a shock tonight, Olena. It's understandable that you'd want to forget about it, put it out of your mind. But this is probably not the best way."

She took another step closer. "Please. Don't treat me like a young, innocent girl. I'm a full-grown woman, if you haven't noticed. And far from innocent."

It was obvious he'd noticed by the way he was looking at her now. His gaze raked over her body, lingering on the swell of her breasts and then her mouth. She took that as an invitation and drew closer to him. They were now only two feet apart. She could feel the heat of his body even from this distance. She could also hear the thumping of his blood in his veins, especially in his neck.

"I know what's good for me and what isn't," she said. "I've lived long enough to accept my regretful moments. And trust me, this won't be one of them."

She didn't wait for his response. Within seconds she breached the distance between them and kissed him. His lips were soft and hot against hers and offered no resistance to her prodding.

He swept his tongue into her mouth and buried his hands in her hair, holding her tight. Sighing, she licked and sucked on his lips and tongue, enjoying the way he tasted. She could clearly taste the danger and the dark in him. It was there hovering on the edge. She wondered how much it would take to push him over it. She'd always been a sucker for a dangerous man, which was why all four of her marriages over the past almost three hundred years had been to men who'd been considered rakes, scoundrels and criminals in their time.

Cale was a different type of dangerous. He was the type of man who could be pushed to his limits, depending on the situation. Pushed to break something, like a moral code, and plunge head-first into something that he never thought he'd ever want. She could sense that in him. And she had a feeling he had a moral code about sleeping with a vampiress.

She could sense the struggle in him as he feasted on her mouth and ran his hands down her hair to her lower back. He quaked beneath her hands as she stroked his smooth, hard flesh. How much would it take to shove him past his principles? A flick of her fingers, a stroke of her hand, a well-placed kiss on some other part of his anatomy? She was willing to find out.

He moaned into her mouth as her hands trailed lower. Her fingers played through the coarse hair around his navel, just as she'd hoped. But when those deft, eager fingers neared the button on his pants, Cale broke away from her kiss.

"Stop," he panted. But the look in his eyes told her he didn't want her to stop. Far from it. She could plainly see the war inside him between what he thought was right and what felt so damn good.

"Are you kidding?" she breathed, hardly able to rein herself in. It took all she had to stop from tearing at the zipper on his trousers. She ached to feel the hot, hard length of him in her hand. To feel the blood thump in his veins.

He covered her hands with his. "This will just make working together complicated."

"Like hell it will." She dropped her hands and stared at him, unable to hide her disappointment. "For you maybe. I'm completely fine with it. It won't affect my work at all."

"Well, I guess you're a lot stronger than I am." He dropped his gaze and went to pick up his shirt still lying on the bed.

"It's because I'm a vampire, isn't it?"

"No, that's not it." He shook his head, but he wouldn't meet her gaze.

She got it now. Complete understanding came to her in a rush of air. He was afraid of her, of what she could do to him if she wanted. He'd been hurt before. She could see it now. Another vampire in another time had hurt Cale.

"I wouldn't hurt you, Cale. I wouldn't take what you don't want to offer."

He looked at her then, and she saw that she'd been right. Some other vampiress had taken from him what he hadn't been willing to give up. She understood that look now. It was full of shame and guilt. As if he'd done something wrong and been punished for it.

She searched his body with her eyes, wondering where he'd been bitten. Not on the neck. She would've seen the marks right away. Not on the wrist, either. Most likely on the inner thigh. It was a good place for both vampire and human. Both would've felt extreme pleasure. Euphoria, even.

"Don't." The one word, spoken with cold, hard control, caused Olena to look up. He'd known what she'd been looking for.

"I'm sorry, Cale. I didn't realize."

"Could you please leave? I'd like to get a couple hours' sleep before we head to the club."

"I'll leave," Olena said, her hands out as if to show him that she was defenseless, harmless. "But I want you to know that I would never do that to you. Never."

He just nodded and continued to button his shirt.

Without another word, Olena turned and left the room. There was nothing she could say to make him believe her. That would take time. Normally, she was not a patient woman when it came to men. But for the first time in a long time, she wanted to wait for this one.

Chapter 8

After Olena left his hotel room, Cale didn't sleep as he'd said he would. He'd lied about being tired. He'd just needed her to leave. The sensations she brought out in him were so intense, they scared him. And her insight into why he was scared freaked him out. She'd hit it right on.

Six years ago he'd met a woman, Marta, during a case—she worked for the agency—and fell headfirst in love with her. Well, maybe it hadn't really been love. Intense, breath-stealing desire most likely. The type of desire that encompassed a person's entire life. That was what it was like with her. Overpowering.

He hadn't known until he was well and thoroughly smitten with her that Marta was a vampiress. By then, he didn't care. He just wanted to be with her all the time. His work even suffered. Richard, his superior, noticed and called him on it. His obsession with her had gotten so deep that Cale had almost quit so he could be with her all the time. Thankfully, he saw the light in time to save his career.

It had been a Friday night, and the two of them were out on a date. They went out for dinner, drinks and dancing, then back to her place. He'd had quite a bit of wine and had been feeling no pain. When they went to bed at her place, Cale had been expecting the usual amazing sex. Marta had been extremely skilled in the bedroom, but the few times before when she'd asked if she could bite him, he had refused.

This time, though, she'd decided not to ask for permission.

During oral sex, she'd bitten him in his femoral artery. At first the pain was immense and he tried to fight her off, but eventually it faded into total bliss. Even now he couldn't really describe the ultimate pleasure he'd felt. But deep down in his soul he'd known he'd been violated. His trust had been shattered.

After Marta had her fill of his blood, he'd rolled off the bed and grabbed his clothes. His vision had been blurred and it felt as if he was very drunk, but he managed to get out of the house and drive back to his place. He hadn't been sure exactly how he'd made it, though. He'd known he'd been weaving all over the road. It still surprised him that someone hadn't gotten hurt by his recklessness. But he had to get away. If he'd stayed in that house, he would've killed Marta.

After that night, Cale never saw her again. She must've known his feelings, because she didn't try to contact him. It was as if the relationship had never happened. He'd stripped his apartment bare of any traces of her. He tossed out all the gifts she'd given him and erased her phone numbers from his home and cell phones.

He dived back into work. He became a better agent. Worked harder, worked longer and never asked for any time off. Richard was at first ecstatic, but after a while, when Cale turned sullen and isolated, he began to worry and told him to get some therapy. But Cale never did. He didn't need it. He was as cured as he was ever going to be.

At least he thought he was.

Being around Olena was bringing up all his feelings from the past. He knew deep down that Olena wasn't Marta. That they were completely different women. But it still didn't stop him from panicking when Olena had kissed him. He couldn't deny he wanted her, but he found it difficult to let down his guard. When her fingers had fluttered at the zipper of his pants, flashes of her fangs digging deep into his thigh had raced through his mind. A shiver had raced down his spine. It was a mixture of fear and excitement. That was what bothered him the most. His conflicted emotions.

They would only get in his way of doing his job. And for Cale, the job was the only thing that mattered anymore.

Once dressed, Cale went into the living area and called room service. He couldn't sleep, but he definitely could eat. He'd need his energy for what was to come. A magical sex club was going to be an interesting experience to say the least.

As he waited for the food to arrive, Cale booted up his laptop. He wanted to do some more research on the victim, Luc Dubois, and his ties to organized crime. He also wanted to know more about Phantasia. There was nothing worse than an awestruck human walking around a place where hungry predators like vampires and lycans lurked. He couldn't go in there appearing weak. They would eat him alive.

While he accessed Interpol's interface, Cale considered all that he'd been able to glean with his telepathy. Olena had been right about the timetable of his arrival. He had already been on the plane to France when the explosion happened at the National Bank of Nouveau Monde.

He'd been working another case, a bomb scare in Paris. There had been a call warning about a bomb on the Eiffel Tower set to blow precisely at noon. The bomb squad had found the bomb and been able to dismantle it just in time. When Cale had inspected the bomb, he got flickers of images in his mind as he touched the wires. He received an image of a vampire, dirty and unkempt, talking about blowing up the bank. And another image of the same guy talking about a virus.

Whoever had constructed the bomb in Paris had something to do with the explosives that took out the safety-deposit boxes in Nouveau Monde.

He might not be the person who did the job, but he'd definitely helped build the mechanism.

Cale had convinced Richard to let him go to Nouveau Monde and investigate further. When he'd mentioned the word *virus,* the Interpol boss got very twitchy. With its catastrophic ramifications, chemical warfare scared everyone inside the agency. But now that Cale was here in the city and saw the destruction in the bank and where it led to, he didn't think this had anything to do with biological weaponry. He had another hunch, but he wasn't quite ready to share that with anyone. Not Richard at Interpol and definitely not Olena.

One o'clock came quickly as he ate and flipped through information on the club and the owners. By the time Olena knocked on his hotel room door, Cale thought he was prepared to enter Phantasia and speak with the people involved.

But once he saw Olena standing in the doorway expectantly, he wished he'd done some preparation to see her again. Despite his reservations about getting involved with her, the sight of her still punched him in the gut. She was a stunner. More beautiful than any woman he'd seen before. And it wasn't just her looks. There was something almost ethereal about her.

"Are you ready to go?" she asked.

He nodded and then turned to get his suit jacket hanging on the back of the chair. Olena had yet to step into the room. He wondered if it was because he hadn't invited her to. He knew that myth about vampires having to be invited was just that—a myth—but he wondered if Olena abided by it to make a point. To give him some sort of control over their partnership. If so, he respected her for that, even if it was purely semantics.

"Here." She thrust out her hand toward him. Hanging from between her fingers was a leather rope with a heavy-looking piece of silver on the end. "You'll need this."

Cale took it. "What is it?"

"It's a charmed amulet for protection. François makes them for the team. He's skilled in defense magic."

"Do I need to worry about going to this club?" He put the necklace over his head. The amulet was weighty and substantial. He could feel warmth emanating from it even through the cotton of his shirt.

She shrugged. "There's always a level of danger when dealing with witches. The powerful ones can be very hard to read. Unpredictable." She said the last bit with a sly smile on her face. She was obviously having a bit of fun at his expense.

"You aren't very funny."

"I know. I'm sorry." She turned to leave. "Are you ready?"

He nodded, and shut the door firmly behind him.

As they walked the hall, Olena regarded him. "Seriously, though, you know that I will have to do most of the talking."

"I know about vampire politics."

"Good." As they neared the elevators, she pressed the down button. "Then we shouldn't have any problems."

The obvious statement shouldn't have given Cale the shivers. But it did. Because he had a feeling that something was going to happen to them at the club. He wasn't exactly sure what, but so far this case and his new partner were becoming more interesting and seriously more dangerous by the second.

Chapter 9

Olena had been to Phantasia only once before. That had been back about sixty years ago, during the Second World War, way before she got involved in crime-scene investigation. The club hadn't been called Phantasia back then, but it had catered to the same clientele, and she imagined still had the same owners. Vampires tended to hold on to things a lot longer than most people. And sentimentality had nothing to do with it. It was always about money and power.

The club was a decadent mixture of fifteenth-century Spanish Inquisition and cabaret. Candles flickered in glass holders fixcd along the rock walls, giving the place both a romantic atmosphere and a spooky one. Red velvet sofas and ornate high-backed chairs decorated with sparkling gems lined the walls and dotted the floor around the stage. Men and women in various types of costume, some almost nude, draped themselves lustfully across the soft, rich fabric of the sofas. They were all under one kind of spell or another. Some came to get high on magic and others to quench their decadent desires. Some both.

There were several black rope trapezes hanging from the high ceilings, every one occupied by either a man or a woman barely clothed in leather or silk. Olena caught Cale's stunned look as his gaze swept the crowded club. When he glanced up and saw the scantily clad woman swinging above him, her blue eyes the only thing visible behind the fanciful mask, his eyes nearly bugged out. If they hadn't been there for such a serious matter, she might've laughed at his reaction. Or taken advantage of it.

For now, she accepted it and tugging on his arm pointed toward the bar. He nodded and followed through the gyrating throng of people. The sounds thumping through the wall-mounted speakers was a mixture of music from around the world. Gaelic verse mixed with African tribal drumming. But what was between the lyrics and rhythm was important. That was where the magic was imbedded.

When they neared the bar, Olena wrapped a hand around the amulet she wore. Silently she thanked François for making them. Because the music seemed extra intense. She could feel tendrils of magic tickling her skin, trying hard to gain entrance into her psyche. She glanced back at Cale and saw the same intense determination on his face. She wondered if he knew exactly what he was fighting.

Partygoers made room at the bar for them. Cale's suit must've given them away. No one came to Phantasia in a suit unless they were police.

She leaned on the counter and stared at the bartender. He tried desperately to ignore her, but when she crooked her finger toward him he obeyed, albeit reluctantly. He shuffled toward her, wiping his hands on a towel.

"What do you want?"

"To talk to whoever is in charge," she said, laying on her power of persuasion. The bartender nearly swooned in her presence, and then he shook his head and pointed toward a red door in the corner of the club.

Olena motioned toward the door. Cale nodded and followed her across the room. As she walked, she glanced over at him and noticed the sweat dripping from his forehead.

She reached for his hand and squeezed it. "Are you okay?"

"I'm fine."

"You're sweating."

"It's hot in here."

She lifted one eyebrow. "Are you sure that's all?"

"Yeah, why else would I be sweating?"

"The magic in here is really powerful. Even I'm feeling it a little." And boy, did she. Her thighs were tingling as if an electrical current was surging through them.

He frowned and tugged his hand out of hers. "Don't worry about me. Let's just do our jobs."

"Fine, but don't say I didn't warn you if you suddenly get the urge to hump something." She smirked.

"Not going to happen."

She knocked on the red door. It opened, and a

big bruiser of a guy stepped out. He was a lycan. Tough as steel and loyal to whom they served, lycans made incredibly tough bodyguards, bouncers and bruisers.

"You have the wrong door," he said.

Cale produced his Interpol badge and flashed it at thc guy. "This is a get-inside-free card. Get me?"

The guard glanced around the room and then opened the door wider, inviting them in. Olena went in first, followed by Cale. The guard shut the door, then swung his beefy arm down the hall, motioning them to walk forward.

Soon they were ushered into another room, a big room with several big people in it. Two more beefy guards stood along one wall, and two men—one was definitely a vampire, the other most likely a witch—sat behind the huge glass-and-chrome desk that dominated the room. They were obviously in charge.

Olena glanced at the dark-haired man, the witch, in the red silk shirt, leaning back in his leather chair. He was smiling and looking very relaxed. She decided to start her questions with him. It might prove to be a safer bet.

She stood in front of the desk, her hands on her hips. "Are you Valentino DeCosta?"

His smile brightened. "In the flesh. And you are?"

"Olena Petrovich of the NMPD. This is Cale Braxton of Interpol. We are here to ask you a few questions about Luc Dubois."

He steepled his fingers on top of the desk. The jewels on his rings flashed in the bright light. "What did Luc do now?"

"He died," Cale answered.

"How?"

"Badly, by the looks of his mutilated body."

Olena glanced over at Cale. He'd not yet taken his eyes off Valentino. She was glad that he understood why she'd started with the witch; that way Cale could get in his licks. When it was the vampire's turn, the agent would have to keep his mouth shut and let her do all the talking.

"So what is it you want to know?"

"Did he have any enemies?"

Valentino smiled. "Of course he did. A long list."

"Would you be included in that list?"

"No. We all loved Luc." He lifted his hands and gestured to the room. "Didn't we?"

All the men in the room laughed at that, except for Otto Krause, the vampire. Olena knew of him.

He was a power-hungry leech trying to make a name for himself in the vampire hierarchy. And he was staring at Cale, a predatory gleam in his dark eyes, as if he was trying to decide which limb of Cale's to rip off first.

"Why is a human Interpol agent in my club?"

Cale visibly stiffened when Otto spoke. Olena realized that his power was probably power-speaking. All vampires had some sort of extra power besides the increased strength, long life, and superior eyesight. She could seduce anyone whenever she wanted. This vamp could probably burst a person's eardrums just by screaming.

Cale was about to say something when Olena braced her hand against his arm to silence him. "He's here with me. Under my protection."

The vampire smiled, and the tips of his fangs distended just a little bit. It was an act of aggression. "You didn't answer my question."

"No, I didn't." Olena smiled right back, baring her own fangs. He was sorely mistaken if he thought he could intimidate her. She'd been around a lot longer than he had. By the smell of him, this vampire was no more than one hundred years old.

Otto leaned forward, eyeing her. "You know,

you look very familiar, Ms. Petrovich. Have you been here before?"

Ignoring the question, Olena asked one of her own to the witch, which she knew was a huge insult to the vampire. "Did Luc have any family? Anyone with access to his home?"

Valentino shook his head. "Not that I'm aware of. If he did, he never spoke of anyone. Luc liked to party, so I imagine there might be tons of people with access to his home."

"Any girlfriends or lovers?"

He smirked. "Who wasn't on his rack one time or another?"

"I don't know. Were you?"

He shook his head and glanced around the room. "Not me, darling."

Olena noticed his gaze lingering a little longer on the vampire.

She turned toward him. "And you, Otto, have you been on Luc Dubois's rack a time or two?"

He moved faster than she'd given him credit for. Within seconds, he'd jumped over the desk and had her pressed up against the wall, his hand wrapped around her throat.

Cale drew his weapon and pointed it at Otto, which sent the room into a panic. All the bodyguards drew their guns and pointed them at Cale and Olena.

"Let her go, mate, or I'll put a silver bullet through your skull," Cale growled.

Otto never took his eyes off of Olena as he snarled, "I'm going to rip out your throat, bitch."

She saw the fury there in his face, but she also saw something else that gave her pause. Sorrow. She'd been right to goad him. This was where the real story was, the real pain. It was obvious to her now that Otto and Luc had been more than just business partners. There was real, honest grief in his dark gaze. He'd had feelings for Luc. Maybe he had even loved him.

"It's all right, Cale. Otto's not going to hurt me. You can put your weapon away."

But Cale wasn't moving. His gun was still pointed at the vampire's head, unwavering, unflinching.

"I wouldn't be so sure of that, bitch."

"Oh, I would." She lifted one eyebrow. "Look down."

Otto glanced down between their bodies and finally noticed the silver blade she had pointed at his heart. The tip was digging into his shirt. His adrenaline was racing so hot and high that he likely hadn't felt it when she drew it from her sleeve and pressed it to his body.

"You see, Otto just wants to talk." She poked him a little harder. "Don't you, Otto?"

He started to laugh, then drew back, releasing his hold on her neck. He ran a shaky hand through his long blond hair and returned to his seat behind the desk.

Cale slowly holstered his gun, never taking his eyes off of the vampire. The guards followed suit and slid theirs away, too.

Olena brushed the front of her shirt. "Now can we get some real answers?"

"Leave us," Otto commanded.

The guards had no choice but to obey. Olena even had the fleeting sense of wanting to leave the room as well. But she planted her feet firmly on the floor, waiting for the bodyguards to leave them alone.

Valentino glanced at Otto with a question in his eyes.

Otto nodded. "You, too, Valentino. Please."

The witch slid out of his chair, came around the desk and followed the bodyguards out. By the look in his eyes, Olena didn't think he was too happy about being dismissed.

Once they were all gone, Olena sat in one of the two visitor's chairs in front of the desk. Cale chose to stand behind her. She kind of liked that he took up that position. A position of authority and protection. He probably had no real clue what his stance was saying. In vampire society, it meant that he was bound to Olena. She smiled, thinking she might let him in on it later. Much later. She was enjoying the turn of events much too much.

"You were right. Luc and I were lovers," Otto confessed.

"I'm sorry for your loss."

His eyes widened in an obvious sign of surprise. "Thank you."

"How long were you together?"

"Twenty-two years."

"Then you would know if Luc had been into something else, something Interpol might have an interest in?" Cale asked.

Olena tried not to flinch, but she was surprised by his outburst, as was Otto by the look on his face. But to his credit he didn't make a big deal out of it. Vampire politics sometimes interfered with what was truly important. Like finding a lover's killer.

Otto shook his head. "Luc didn't talk about

some of his dealings, and I didn't press him. I loved him. I didn't own him. He could come and go as he pleased."

"But he was into something besides part ownership of his club and several others around the city?"

"Yes."

"Any inkling of what that might be?" Olena asked.

"Computers, maybe. I overheard him one night on the phone talking about servers and networks. I'm clueless about that tech stuff, so it could've been anything."

"Do you know of anyone who would want him dead?"

Otto shook his head. "Valentino is right. We all have enemies. You don't work in the underworld and not have them. But Luc was well liked and well respected. I don't know of anyone who would cross those lines."

Olena stood. "Thank you, Otto. You've been helpful."

"I wish I could tell you more."

"We'll find whoever killed Luc."

He nodded, but looked weary, as if his lover's death had taken a chunk of his life as well. Olena thought maybe it had. Sometimes that happened when vampire mates died. The death left a permanent hole in the other's heart, in their psyche, in their soul. One that could never be filled again. This was one of the reasons Olena never took on a vampire mate. Losing a loved one was bad enough, but losing a piece of oneself as well was too much.

Cale was silent as they left the office. Olena glanced back at him. He looked at her as if he wanted to say something, but he didn't open his mouth. She wondered what he was thinking. He was definitely a difficult man to read. She could usually tell what most men were thinking—human, vampire or lycan. But Cale was a tough nut to crack. Maybe his telepathy came with a psychic shield to protect himself.

They walked down the hall to the red door. Valentino seemed to be waiting for them. When they approached, the witch smiled. He was an affable-looking man, but there was something about him that sent a rush of cold shivers down Olena's back.

"I hope you got what you came for," he said.

"I hope we did as well," Olena responded. "If not, we'll be back."

"I'll be looking forward to that." He bowed his head a little, then offered his hand to Cale.

Cale took it but it was a cautious move. He was right to be cautious. The witch was a manipulator.

Just then the door opened and one of the big bruisers came rushing through. He ran into Valentino, which in turn pushed him forward into Olena and Cale. He wrapped his arms around them both to keep from falling. Olena set him back onto his feet.

"Damn it, Jake!" Valentino bellowed at the bodyguard. "Watch what you're doing."

Jake had the presence of mind to look sheepish and hung his head like an old hound dog. "Sorry, Val."

"I apologize for my brutish employee." He swung his hand toward the open door. "I will bid you both a fond farewell."

Olena went out the door. Cale followed. The music had changed, and the club was even more packed now, the gyrating mob harder to get through than before.

She pushed past the sweaty, dancing people, trying to make it to the exit. Halfway across the floor, she started to feel different. The air felt heavier, as if it pressed down around her, making it more difficult to move.

Her skin started to itch. She glanced down at her arms and noticed her hair standing to attention and sweat beading her flesh. Licking her lips, she glanced around her. The lights seemed to be dancing around her, playing a game of tag. And she was it.

Magic. She could feel it penetrating her pores. Sweat rolled down her back. Something deep within her belly started to flutter. The sensation traveled lower still, until the ache between her thighs became unbearable.

She turned to say something to Cale when he grabbed her arm hard. Sweat was pouring down his face, and he was licking his lips nervously, just as she had done. "I'm feeling a little strange, Olena."

It was then she noticed his missing amulet. Panicked, she reached up to her neck for hers. But it was also gone.

Valentino must've slipped them off when he fell into them in the corridor. They were in a lot of trouble. If they didn't get out of there soon, they would be pulled under by the sexual spell. And who knew what would happen then?

Chapter 10

A rush of adrenaline surged through Cale. He felt not only light-headed, but giddy with it. By the stunned expression on Olena's face it was obvious the magic in the room was affecting them both.

"Our amulets are gone," she said. "We need to get out of here."

She grabbed his hand to pull him through the crowd on the dance floor. The moment her skin touched his, he felt a lightning bolt of power zing through him. It went from the tips of his fingers to the tips of his toes, making all the parts in between tingle. The sensation exhilarated and frightened him at the same time. Especially since he had an insatiable urge to pull Olena to him and crush his mouth to hers.

He wanted to bury his hands in her hair and kiss her hard and long. The thought of her tongue dancing against his made him instantly hard. So hard that he found it a little bit difficult to walk. His legs were shaking, as was the rest of his body. Shivers of hot desire made his flesh quiver and sweat. And he wanted to press his slick body to Olena's. He wanted her so much. He could hardly breathe from the explosiveness of it. He had a crushing urge to drop to his knees and bury his face into her flesh.

He knew it was the magic making him feel this way. But he also knew that those feelings of desire and want had already been there. The spell was just amplifying them. It was so overpowering, he could barely resist it. As they managed to cross the floor, he was hanging on to his sanity.

When they reached the door, Cale gritted his teeth against the violent urges. But it was too much; he couldn't control his hunger any longer. Maybe just a taste would sate him enough to continue.

Yanking Olena to a stop, Cale grabbed her by the shoulders and pushed into a shadowed nook by the door. He slammed her up against the wall and ground his body into hers.

Her eyes widened, darkened, but she didn't protest when he crushed his mouth to hers. In fact, her lips parted and she moaned as he kissed her. Her hands fisted in his shirt and it was as if she was holding onto him to keep from falling.

She tasted like a hot, humid day at the beach. Sultry and salty. Warm and languid. God, if only he could feast on her all night, maybe then his hunger would abate. But as it was, it was growing fiercer, more violent by the second.

He wrapped his hands in her hair, reveling in the way the silky strands caressed his skin. He pulled on it to bring her closer to him. Grinding himself into her, he let her know just how hard and hot she was making him.

She moaned and mimicked his motions, which made him even hotter and hard as steel.

His restraint was fraying. He clamped his eyes shut against it and pulled his mouth from hers. She groaned in protest.

"I can't hold on much longer," he grunted.

"We have to get outside," she panted as her

hands spread across his chest and began to massage him through the fabric.

"I don't think I can let go of you," he said through gritted teeth.

"Don't then." She lifted a leg and wrapped it around his waist. "Lift me up and carry me outside."

Burying his face into her neck, Cale let his hands slip down her body. He skimmed his fingers past her breasts. He felt her flinch and quiver at his light touch. He groaned, biting down on his lip as he wrapped his hands around her round, firm derriere. Slowly, torturously, he lifted her up so both her legs could fit snugly around his waist. But the movement forced her pelvis to tilt up and he could feel the heat of her center nuzzled against his groin.

This wasn't going to be easy. Not when he wanted to rip off her pants and plunge into her right there and then. He knew she'd be hot and wet and open for him. He could already feel the warm, damp desire against his trousers.

"Hurry, Cale," she murmured against his ear.

Digging his fingers into the flesh of her rear end, Cale carried her out of the dark alcove and toward the door. The friction of her groin against his nearly brought him down, but after two more steps he was able to kick the door open and carry her out into the brisk early-morning air.

He thought for sure he'd feel the relief instantly. But he didn't. Desire, hot and hard, still ran rampant through his system like heroin. He'd never felt a more potent drug than Olena.

"I don't feel any change."

She squirmed in his arms and moaned against his neck. "Maybe we need to get farther away from the club."

Cale ran toward the car. When he reached it, he set Olena onto the hood. That was a mistake. Now his hands were free to roam elsewhere.

"The keys are in my pocket," she panted, and leaned back against the hood to allow him access to her front pants pocket.

That was another mistake. Because now to Cale it looked like she was offering herself to him. He looked down at her parted, swollen mouth and couldn't help but take another taste of her.

When his mouth covered hers, she responded in kind, wrapping her hands in his hair and locking him tight to her. The heels of her shoes dug into the backs of his thighs, and she slid a little forward. Enough that their bodies were touching again.

"Damn it, woman. You're killing me," he groaned against her lips.

"I'm sorry," she whispered, "I can't help it." And then gripping his hair tight, she kissed him again, sweeping her tongue over his.

His hands had been braced against the car hood, but now he moved them over her, seeking her, filling themselves with her generous breasts. Her nipples were hard and rigid, and he rubbed his thumbs over them, wondering what reaction he could get from her if he ran his tongue and teeth over them instead.

"Lower," she groaned, "move your hands lower. To my pocket."

He glanced down between them, to the crotch of her pants. He had the sudden vision of tearing the seam in half and sliding his fingers into her slick warmth. He thought about how she would feel inside, how she would squirm and moan as he manipulated her hard and fast.

"I don't think that's a good idea." He nibbled on her bottom lip, intrigued by the way the tips of her fangs scraped his top lip. He wondered how she could control the urge for blood at a time like this. If it had been reversed and he was a vampire, he wasn't sure he'd have that kind of restraint.

"Do it. It's our only chance to escape this." She licked his lips and then the side of his jaw up to his ear. "This isn't how you want me, is it? You want it to be on your terms, don't you?"

Her words penetrated his fog of euphoria and prompted him into action. He did want her, desperately, but not like this. Well, like this maybe, with her pinned underneath him, but not because of a magic spell. He didn't need any spell to want to bury himself in her.

Closing his eyes and biting down on his lip, he streaked his hand down to her leg, careful not to touch her where he wanted to most. His fingers searched for her pocket, found it, and squirmed inside to retrieve the keys. Once he had the ring around his finger he pulled them out, dangling them in front of her eyes like a prize.

"Good," she said. "Now we just have to get into the car."

He shook his head to clear it. Was he starting to feel the magic fade? He couldn't be sure, but for the last thirty seconds, he'd been able to concentrate on something other than burying himself deep inside Olena. There was hope at least.

"On the count of three, push me away," he told her.

"I don't know if I can." She kissed his chin again, and then licked his lips.

He kissed her. He couldn't deny himself. Not when the taste and feel of her was like ambrosia. After a thorough taste, he pulled away and rested his forehead against hers.

"You can, luv. Just remember what an ass I am."

"You are an ass." She reached around and squeezed the flesh of his buttocks. "And you have an amazing one as well."

That made him laugh, and he could feel the tendrils of magic unraveling. He just needed a little more restraint and he'd be able to take his hands off her amazing body. It would be hard, but he needed to do it. If they succumbed to their desire now, it would ruin their working relationship. But even as he knew that, accepted that, it was damn near impossible for him not to kiss her again or touch her on every rise and slope of her fine form.

Leaning down, he framed her face with his hands, gently stroking her hair. He kissed her, a light brushing of his lips. "I want to give in to the spell and have you. I ache so bad for you. But we both know it would be a mistake that couldn't be fixed."

"I know," she said.

"Push me away, Olena. I don't have the power to do it on my own."

Clamping her eyes shut, she kicked him with her legs. The movement sent him sprawling backward and he had to put his hands out to the sides to keep from falling over. But the second he was separated from her, his head started to clear. He could almost think straight. Almost. The sight of her, doe-eyed and sprawled out on top of the hood sent sparks of heat zinging all over his body. He was still as hard as stone.

Olena also seemed to be breathing easier. She sat up on the hood, tucked her hair behind her ear and let out a loud sigh. "We're not out of the woods yet, but I think we'll make it."

He handed her the car keys. "You drive. I don't think I can." He glanced down at himself. The crotch of his trousers was bulging.

He realized his blunder at making notice of it when her gaze settled there and another rush of heat swelled over him.

She licked her lips. He had a sense that she was

going to jump on him, tackle him to the ground, but instead she stood and went around the side of the car to the driver's door.

He followed her lead and got into the passenger side.

She buckled in, started the engine and put it in gear. "Hang on. This is going to be one fast ride."

Chapter 11

The drive to Cale's hotel took all of ten minutes. Olena drove way over the speed limit, using the vehicle's police lights to get them through the intersections. Thankfully, there wasn't much traffic this early in the morning. She didn't want to be accused of abusing her authority for her own selfish needs.

Although her needs were just about killing her by the time she pulled up in front of the hotel doors.

Sweat had soaked her entire body, and she'd driven with the window down. Anything to keep her mind alert and off the sexy, delicious man in the passenger seat.

It took all she had to keep her hands on the steering wheel and off his remarkably powerful body. She had felt every single muscle and ridge of him when he'd had her pinned to the hood of the vehicle. Although deep down she knew it was wrong, forced by magic, she had wanted it, wanted him so badly she didn't think she could survive without his touch. Without him taking her right there and then.

But she hadn't perished. They were both now sitting in the car in front of his hotel. But neither one of them had made a move since.

She glanced over at Cale. His fingers were pressing into his legs. She could see the quiver in his arms and the twitch along his jawline. She had to fight the urge to reach over and smooth down that line, to unfurl his fingers and entwine them with hers.

She bit down on her lip. The taste of blood exploded on her tongue. It relieved her insatiable hunger temporarily.

"I should get out of the car." He looked at her and she could see the rapid need in his gaze. It made her body quiver even more.

She kept his gaze, not wanting to lose the intensity of the power zinging between them. The energy brushed over her, giving her gooseflesh. She shivered, then dropped her gaze.

"Yeah, you should," she was finally able to say.

Without another word, Cale opened the door and slid out. She didn't watch him while he walked into the hotel. She couldn't and still be able to drive away. The spell was slipping, but it was all the other feelings, the authentic ones she harbored for him, that made her want to shout at him through the window to get back into the car and finish what they'd started.

But she stomped her foot on the gas pedal and drove away.

Only when she pulled up to her high-rise apartment building did she relieve the pressure. As quickly as she could, she put the car in park, grabbed her bag and almost ran to the front door. She tossed the keys to the valet who always parked her cars. Peter grabbed them on the fly and didn't say anything to her. She never gave him a chance, anyway.

The doorman, a large, imposing lycan, quickly opened the door for her. "Good morning, Ms. Petrovich."

"Leo," she said as she swept through the door and toward the elevators. She pressed the up button, cursing under her breath that it was so damn slow.

Finally it arrived and the door slid open. She went in and pushed the button for her floor, then pressed the close button several times. "Come on. Come on."

"Hold the door, please," came a heavily accented voice from the foyer.

Olena saw the wrinkled and withered face of Mrs. Edda Jacobs come into view just as the door closed. She shrugged at the old witch. "Sorry, Edda."

The door closed before she could hear what the cranky old bird said in response. She imagined it wouldn't have been anything complimentary. The two of them had never gotten along in all the years that they both lived in the high-rise. Besides, what was an old woman like Edda doing out this early in the morning? It was barely 3:00 a.m.

The elevator couldn't go fast enough. By the time it arrived at the twenty-fifth floor, Olena was impatiently tapping her foot and clenching her jaw tightly. When the door slid open she rushed out and ran to her door. She stuck the key in and threw open the door. Tossing everything onto the floor, she made a dash to the bathroom. Her white Persian cat chased after her down the hall.

She entered the bathroom, and after throwing open the shower stall's door, she wrenched on the water taps. Bitter-cold water instantly rushed out. Her cat weaved her way through Olena's legs, trying to get her attention.

"Not now, Marie." Olena stripped off her clothes in one swoop, then jumped into the shower.

The icy water bit into her flesh like razor blades. "Ah, gods. That's cold," she shrieked. But she didn't make a move to either step out of the shower or alter the temperature.

An ice-cold shower was the perfect cure for a sexual spell.

She stood under the arctic spray until her fingers, toes and every inch of skin was numb. Finally, she couldn't feel the magic skimming the surface of her body, wriggling its way through her pores. She'd washed it away.

But no matter how much water she sprayed over her flesh, she could still feel the press of Cale's lips on hers and the touch of his hands.

That was something she didn't think she'd ever rinse away.

The man was way more potent than any outside magical enchantment. Not even the most talented and proficient witch could sway her as much as he had.

She turned off the taps and stepped out into a huge terry cloth towel, heated by the towel rack. Marie meowed at her from her perch on the counter by the sink.

Olena scratched the cat's head. "Hello, little lady."

The cat meowed again, sounding quite indignant, as she stretched up toward Olena's fingers.

"Sorry for ignoring you. But it was important. Trust me."

She dried her body off, slid on her emerald-green robe, then gathering Marie in her arms, went into the kitchen. She needed some sustenance. The spell and its effects had wiped her of her energy. Hovering on the brink of release and not finding it was hell on a vampire's system.

She opened the refrigerator and took out a bottle of blood. After twisting the cap off, she drained it in two greedy gulps. She set the empty down on the counter and wiped her mouth with the back of her hand.

Marie meowed again, and pawed at the bottle.

Olena smiled. "No. You can't have any of that. But I will get you some breakfast."

She opened the cupboard to get the cat some food. Marie had been her only companion for a long time, thirty-some years. The Persian wasn't a miracle cat. She'd just ingested a few drops of vampire blood at birth and now was very long-lived. Thankfully, she hadn't inherited any of the other vampire genes. The thought of Marie drinking a saucer filled with O negative almost turned Olena's stomach.

She was setting Marie's food on the floor when a knock came at her door.

Startled, Olena pulled the tie on her robe tighter. Who could be at her door? No one could come up without first being phoned in.

Nerves shot up her spine, giving her an uneasy feeling. When she got to her door, she peered through the peephole. Valentino stood there, grinning happily.

"I know you're there, Olena."

She opened the door. "How did you get up here?"

"Invisibility spell. Quite simple really." He said it with a prideful sneer. As if she'd be impressed with his trespassing.

"You have about two seconds to turn around and leave before I do something ridiculously painful to you."

"I have information for you."

"Why didn't you give it to me before you deliberately spelled me and Agent Braxton into almost screwing on the hood of my car?"

He put a hand to his chest as if she'd insulted him. "I didn't spell you. The club is a magic sex club, Olena. Just coming into the place put you at risk."

She raised one eyebrow, not buying his story one bit.

"Besides I didn't want to be seen giving you this information. Otto can be quite vicious when it comes to Luc's affairs."

"Affairs, as in sexual encounters or business dealings?"

"Both."

She glared at him for another few seconds before giving him a nod. "Fine. You have two minutes." She opened the door wider for him to enter.

As he stepped into her apartment, his gaze swept the front foyer. "Nice. I didn't realize you were this wealthy."

She glared at him. "I've lived a long time. Money is just one of the many things I've collected along the way."

"Men being one of the others?"

"You now have one minute and thirty seconds. Start talking." She shut the door but never took her eyes off him. "And keep your hands in your pockets. I don't want to find one of your juju bags full of whatever spells lying on my floor after you've left."

"Wouldn't dream of doing something like that."

"Uh-huh." She crossed her arms over her chest and stared at him. "What's the information?"

"Luc does have some family around. A niece."

"And?"

"I know that Otto doesn't like her."

"So?"

"Well, if you check Luc's will, I'm sure it will say that he's left everything to her and not to his longtime lover and friend, Otto."

"Including his interest in your little magic sex club?"

He nodded.

Interesting. The information definitely went toward motive, and Otto definitely had means. But what did it have to do with Interpol? What would be their interest in a simple robbery and murder?

"Do you have a name, address?"

"Ivy Seaborn. Not sure where she lives. She's only seventeen, but I believe she lives out on her own. Both parents are dead. Luc was her only family as well."

"Is she vampire?"

He shook his head. "Dhampir. From what I hear she's pretty powerful in magic."

"Sounds like you're jealous."

He sneered, and in his eyes she could see something dark. It was there for a moment and then vanished. "Not likely."

She nodded, but she didn't believe him. He was jealous. Either of this teen's power or of something else.

Olena opened her door. "Time's up. Thanks for the information."

Grinning, he walked back to the door, but hesitated in the threshold. "You know, I remember you from the club."

"I don't think so."

"Yes, I remember it well. Nineteen forty-two. I was only a teenager then. But I can still recall a Russian beauty performing on the stage. It was the most erotic scene I've ever had the privilege of watching. It still fuels some of my dreams." He eyed her up and down. She had the sense that he was trying to see through her robe.

She frowned, trying hard not to wrap her arms around her body. She didn't want to give him the satisfaction. "That was over sixty years ago."

He waved a hand in front of his face. "Longevity spell. I have a lot of power as well, Olena. I'm not simply a sex-magic conjurer."

"I'll have to remember that." She would remember that about him, and more. On the surface Valentino seemed genial and polite, but she didn't think for one moment that his visit to her home was anything but rife with ulterior motives.

He stepped through the door, but before she could shut it on him, he put a hand out. "I wonder what your friends at the police would think about your depraved tryst at Phantasia. You put on quite a show."

Olena just laughed. "Please, I've worked in

the French court of Marie Antoinette. I have done far more decadent things." She shut the door and locked it.

Valentino was kidding himself if he thought he had something to hold over her. Olena had been around long enough to not harbor guilt over what she'd done in the past. It just took too much time and energy to stress over the past. Especially since she had so much of it to stress over. Nearly three hundred years was a long time to exist while worrying about past transgressions. Besides that, her friends at the lab knew her well enough to know that there were some things she was never going to share with them. And that was fine with them. They had skeletons in their own closets. That's what made it so interesting to be working with them, she thought.

Padding into the other room, she snagged the cordless phone from a side table and punched in Gabriel's cell number. He answered on the third ring.

"Bellmonte."

"I have some new information about Luc Dubois."

"Your trip to the club went well, then?" She could hear something odd in his voice.

"Were you sleeping?" she asked.

"Nope. Just resting my eyes."

She glanced at the clock on the wall. It was four-thirty. She mentally smacked herself in the head. Gabriel usually didn't start his shift until six. She was usually on the night shift, coming into work at four in the afternoon and working until four in the morning or later. But this case needed more than her usual twelve-hour shift.

"I'm sorry, Gabriel. I didn't realize what time it was."

"Don't worry about it." She could hear him moving around, probably sitting up and reaching for his omnipresent pen and notepad. "What did you get?"

"Luc Dubois has a young niece. Ivy Seaborn. We need to run a search on her and get an address. She's the recipient of his fortune."

"Maybe his lawyer will have the particulars. I'll put a call in right away."

"All right. Thanks."

"So, how's it going with Agent Braxton? Are you playing nice with him?"

At the words, Olena remembered stroking her hands up and down Cale's chest. Remembered his lips making their way down her chin to her neck.

Her heart picked up a beat just thinking about it. Oh, yeah, she was playing real nice.

"Yeah, everything's fine. He's not so bad."

There was silence on Gabriel's end. Then he sighed. "Why do I get the feeling there's something going on that I most likely don't want to know about?"

"Probably because there is."

He sighed again, more heavily this time. "Okay. I'll see you at the lab."

"I'll be there in a couple of hours. I need a catnap."

She hung up and went into her bedroom. She flung the robe off and padded across the thick ivory rug to the king-size platform bed. Flinging the duvet aside, Olena slid into the comfort of the cotton sheets. She nestled her head onto the pillow and closed her eyes. She just needed a good hour of sleep and she'd feel rested and ready to go again.

Except when she closed her eyes, images of Cale popped up. Cale grinning down at her, his hands molding her breasts, his eyes dark and dangerous. The tip of his tongue peeking out to lick his bottom lip. Every single thought of him was sexual in nature. Every single one. She was doomed.

She opened her eyes again and sighed. Despite the fact that she'd washed away the spell, she was still fully aroused. But the last thing she could do was sate herself with Cale. He was hands off. At least for now.

Chapter 12

Cale had stood in a cold shower for at least an hour. By the time he got out, his skin was wrinkled and he had uncontrollable shakes. But at least he didn't have an erection. It had thankfully gone down after the first half hour. The next half hour under the icy shower spray was to make sure it stayed down.

Wrapped in a terry cloth robe and drinking hot black coffee, he sat on the sofa in his hotel room and dialed the number to Richard, his superior at Interpol. It rang five times before anyone answered.

"Alcott," came a muffled male voicc.

"Did I wake you?"

"As the matter of fact you did, Braxton. It better be important."

"I need you to run a couple of names through the special case files."

"You really didn't need to call me this damn early for that." He sighed. "Why can't you call them yourself?"

"You know why."

"Ah, right. Sorry. I forgot."

Marta worked in the special cases section of Interpol. This was the place that gathered and compiled extensive dossiers on Otherworlders known to be involved with crime. That was how they had met, working a case.

"What are the names?" Richard asked.

"Luc Dubois, Otto Krause and Valentino DeCosta." Cale sipped his coffee. "I need everything on them. Business dealings, known associates, family lineage."

"What do you have going there? Armed robbery, extortion, what?"

"Not sure yet. But I know there are a bunch of people involved."

"Vampires?"

"And others."

"Okay, I'll get these names to Marta and call you when I have something. Call me if you need any more help."

"Thanks, Richard." Cale shut his cell phone and set it on the table. Taking his cup, he sat back in the overstuffed sofa and considered all the leads he had.

It didn't take long because he didn't have much. Just bits and pieces. Images of a bomb, which he'd gleaned from touching a piece of wire during another case, a group of vampires, a young woman with bright blue eyes. Nothing much when put all together. But after talking with Valentino and Otto at the club, he knew that either man or both were involved somehow. It was something to do with Luc and his business dealings. And not the legal ones.

Whatever was in his safety-deposit box at the time of the explosion was the key. Luc Dubois had been in possession of something that was worth a bundle. Something worth killing him over. After working so many cases, Cale knew it was almost always about money and power. No matter what species, people were motivated by only a few things—anger, lust and greed.

Lust. Now there was something he was getting right up close and personal with. He knew all about that one. Even now, without a sex spell, his thoughts of Olena turned carnal. It was difficult not to think about the woman in reference to sex. Not with her full, pouty mouth and luscious body. And he with his hands full of her generous breasts barely an hour ago. It was enough to make a grown man cry.

If he could go back in time to the club, he wasn't sure if he would've agreed to let her go. He knew it had been the right thing for them to resist the temptation of the spell, but he wasn't happy about it. Giving in to it would've been a much better plan in his mind. He'd certainly be a lot happier.

Cursing under his breath, Cale set the coffee cup down on the table and lay back on the sofa. He needed a couple of hours of sleep, then he'd be able to get back into work. The sooner he could solve this thing, the sooner he could move on. And the sooner he could forget about Olena Petrovich.

When he got back to the lab, he still had Olena firmly on his mind. It didn't help that the moment he saw her in Gabriel's office, his body clenched in response.

She avoided his gaze as he entered the office. He nodded to Gabriel, who was sitting on the edge of his desk.

"Get some sleep, Agent Braxton?"

"Not much." He risked a glance at Olena. She was looking at Gabriel, but by the faint smudges under her amazing eyes it looked as if she hadn't gotten much rest, either. He was smug enough to enjoy that a little.

"Olena's gotten some new information that has given us a good lead."

Cale swiveled around to look at her. "When did this happen?"

She moved out of the shadows and came to sit in one of the visitor chairs in front of Gabriel's desk. "I had a visitor."

Her fluid movements gave Cale a whiff of her alluring perfume. It took all he had to not take in another noseful.

"Who?"

"Valentino."

"That snake," he growled.

She nodded. "That was my thought as well."

"What did he tell you?"

"The name of Luc's nicce. Ivy Seaborn."

Gabriel opened the file in his hand. "I was able to get a copy of the victim's will and it names Ms. Seaborn the heir."

"She gets it all?" Cale asked.

Gabriel nodded. "Everything."

"I wonder how the boys feel about that."

"From what I could sense from Valentino, he wasn't too happy," Olena said. "But he was even more thrilled to inform me that Otto wasn't happy, either, since he expected to be named in Luc's will."

"It doesn't work as a motive to kill him, though. It wouldn't make any sense, especially since the girl would get everything."

"No, it doesn't," Gabriel interjected. "And what, if anything, does it have to do with the safety-deposit box at the bank?"

"We need to track down this niece," Cale said. Thoughts of the girl with the piercing blue eyes flashed in his mind. He wondered if this was part of his vision.

Olena produced a piece of paper and waved it in the air. "Done. Got her address."

"Luc Dubois's lawyer has tried to contact Ms. Seaborn, but with no luck," Gabriel added. "So she may not even know her uncle is dead."

"Well, I guess she's about to find out. Let's go, then. Daylight's awasting." Cale headed for the door, then stopped and glanced back at Olena. "Is the sun going to be a bother?"

Standing, she smirked at him. "Nope. That's what cool, expensive sunglasses are for." She produced a pair and she slid them on.

He smiled, pleased that their tense situation had passed. And hell yes, she looked damn fine in those expensive sunglasses.

Chapter 13

Ivy Seaborn lived in a bad part of town. Graffiti marked decrepit, dilapidated buildings. Garbage lined the gutters of every street. And the homeless made their nests in alleys and in doorways long unused.

It saddened Olena that there was poverty and homelessness in a city like Nouveau Monde. But, she supposed, just because someone was vampire, lycan or witch didn't make him necessarily immune from life's hardships. Otherworlders had their fair share of junkies, too. Humans weren't the only ones who had addictions.

As Olena parked the car along one desolate street, she wondered how Ivy had ended up in a place like this. Especially with an uncle as wealthy as Luc Dubois. According to Valentino, they had been close. Close enough that Luc left everything to her.

It was just another mystery on top of many so far on this case.

The address was for one of those rent-by-the-week hotels. The ones where the bathroom was down the hall and almost always had roaches and smelled like someone had died in it recently. As Olena and Cale made their way through the dark and dingy lobby, Olena had the utmost pleasure of being flashed by an eighty-year-old lycan still half formed in his wolfish self.

He ran up to her, from where she couldn't say, opened his long dirty trench coat, flashed her a winning smile, then dashed out of the way before Cale could grab him. He'd been quick for an old man. Obviously his lycan reflexes were still in good form. Too bad the rest of him hadn't been.

Cale shook his head after the old man had escaped. "That was quite disturbing."

"He didn't wiggle his you-know-what at *you.* *I* received the full show."

He laughed, and the hearty sound of it made Olena join in. After what had happened, she'd thought for sure that there would be nothing but tension between them. And not the good kind, either.

But they were back to normal. She was glad. She liked Cale, liked being around him. She didn't want that to change.

Their attention returned to the stairs leading up to the five floors of the hotel. "What floor is she on?" he asked.

"Third. Room 308."

When they mounted the stairs, Cale's nose wrinkled. "What is that smell?"

"Rotting meat, I think. I imagine most of the tenants here are lycans. There are far more wealthy vampire and witch families than lycan. Partly because of longevity and partly because most lycans don't possess greed and a lust for power."

"Interesting."

"There are a ton of books out on the subject."

They made the second floor and were heading up the next set of stairs. Olena wished she'd worn gloves as her hand touched a sticky substance on the handrail.

"What about you, then?"

She glanced at him. "What about me?"

"Longevity or greed and lust for power?"

"I've been around for almost three hundred years and still choose to work for a living. What do you think?"

"I think you're…" He paused.

"What?"

"A good investigator. And you strive to make a difference."

She arched an eyebrow. "Do I hear some begrudging respect in there somewhere?"

"Yeah, but it's not begrudging. It's honest."

She looked at him then, really looked. His gaze was intense but not with the usual desire-laced darkening. It told her volumes about how he was starting to feel about her. There was respect, which he had already admitted to, and more. But she wasn't quite sure what that more entailed. She wasn't ready to dissect it quite yet, because then she'd have to investigate her own feelings toward Cale.

She understood lust, desire, even friendship, but she wasn't sure she could handle anything else. Not from this man, anyway. Because she knew it wouldn't be casual, wouldn't be cavalier. It would be serious and intense. And she wasn't ready for that.

Clearing her throat, she waved her hand toward a dark and dirty hallway. "I think it's that way."

After carefully adjusting his tie, Cale nodded and followed her down the corridor.

Olena reached room 308 and knocked on the door. There was no immediate answer, so she tried again. Still nothing. She put her ear to the chipped wooden door but heard no movement inside. Ivy wasn't home.

"Do we have a work address?" Cale asked.

Olena shook her head. "This is all we could get from the lawyer. Nothing turned up in any of our databases, either. She doesn't have a criminal record."

"We could ask around. Maybe someone knows where she works or goes during the day."

"It's worth a try."

They returned to the lobby hoping someone was manning the front desk. It turned out there was. An old, grizzled looking vampire named Bartholomew, Bart to his friends.

Olena leaned on the counter. "Ivy Seaborn. Room 308. Do you know her?"

"I know 308. No Ivy living there."

"Are you sure?"

He nodded, seemingly more interested in picking the dirt from under his long, ragged nails. "A guy named Tick. He pays me in cash. That's all I know."

"Do you know where this Tick works?" Cale asked.

Bart shrugged. "Try the comic shop down the street. I know he reads a lot of those."

They thanked Bart and headed back out onto to the street to find this comic-book store. Olena glanced one way, Cale the other.

"Shouldn't be too hard to find," she said. "There aren't too many businesses open down here."

"You lead, I'll follow."

Olena smiled. "I like the sound of that."

"I thought you would."

Olena walked east down the street. After two blocks they found the comic-book store. Cale pushed open the door for Olena. The little bell overhead chimed, announcing their arrival.

It was dark, musty and smoky. Olena waved her hand in front of her face to get rid of the sweet odor of marijuana and the haze that blinded her. Squinting, she looked around the shop. She spotted a young guy sitting on the counter by the cash register reading a comic; she thought he probably worked here. And there was another young man in the corner pawing through a huge stack of comics.

She glanced at Cale. He seemed to understand exactly what she was thinking, because he went toward the guy in the corner while she went toward the one on the counter.

Olena flipped open her law enforcement badge and held it up beside her face. "Which one of you is Tick?"

The young man on the counter glanced at the guy in the corner. The guy Olena suspected was the one and only Tick. And that was all it took to set everything in motion.

Tick pushed the stack of comics aside, and leaping over a shelf of graphic novels, headed toward the back of the shop.

"Damn it! I didn't think he'd run," Olena said even as she sprinted across the shop floor. Cale was right on her heels. As she ran through the torn-open back door, she glanced over her shoulder. "Think you can keep up?"

"Don't worry about me. I'm human, but I'm quick on my feet."

"Yeah, well, we'll soon see." She looked down the alleyway and saw Tick heading around the corner. She had a suspicion he was a lycan, hence the clever name. "If he shifts, we won't have a chance."

Without another word, she started down the alley, full sprint. She wasn't a good runner, but she was faster than an average human male. Except maybe for Cale. He seemed to be keeping up with her just fine. But in no way did she find the man average, so it didn't surprise her.

After two blocks, they lost Tick. He was fast and agile and obviously very good at hiding.

"Where do you think he went?" Cale asked, slightly doubled over, breathing hard.

Olena scanned the streets. "Ducked into one of these buildings maybe. They all look abandoned."

"Do you want to keep looking?"

She nodded. "Yes. We need to find Ivy."

"Okay."

Side by side, they searched the first building. It was mostly empty except for a few squatters happily shooting up their drug of choice. It didn't take them too long to search the three floors, but they came up with nothing.

When they exited that building and were

walking to the next, Olena heard music coming from another abandoned building. She motioned in the direction of the sound. "Let's check over there. I hear techno music."

Cale followed her across the street to the other building. When she neared, she could see that the front door had been torn open. It was still swinging in the slight breeze.

The moment they entered the building, the music became louder, clearer. It definitely was some sort of techno. She could hear other things as well. Voices.

As they crept up the stairwell, Cale stopped her with a hand on her arm. "Be careful," he said. "We don't know how many people there might be."

She nodded, touched by his concern. He was an odd one for sure. Here he was likely the only human within miles, completely outmatched without any super powers, and he was worried about her. The fact that he was said a lot about him and his character. Character she was really starting to like a lot.

When they reached the first-floor landing, Olena could see flashing light down one long hallway. Maybe they'd stumbled across an underground rave. There were many around the city.

Raves were not considered illegal per se, but what happened during them usually was—drug use and underage drinking.

She nudged Cale with her elbow and pointed down the hall. He nodded and without a word followed her lead.

Walking tall, fangs out, Olena walked down the hall, which opened up into a large room that she imagined was once an office space. Loud music thumped out of the multitude of speakers lining the walls. A DJ was up on a makeshift platform spinning his tunes. There was a small crowd dancing, maybe fifteen teens, like awestruck zombies in the middle of the room, every single one with a drink in their hand.

Olena's gaze swept the room looking for Tick. She found him in the corner crouched on a beat-up old sofa. He was talking animatedly to a young girl with spiky white-blond hair and multiple facial piercings.

As she moved farther into the room, with Cale behind her, people started to shift out of her way. By the time they reached the middle, pretty much everyone was aware of their presence.

Tick's head came up and his eyes widened.

The girl beside him also started. She rose to her feet, her vivid blue eyes as wide as saucers.

Cale grabbed Olena's arm and nodded toward the girl. "That's her. That's Ivy. I saw her in one of my visions."

Chapter 14

The girl must've either overheard him or sensed that they were looking for her, because she bolted. Tick went one way, she went the other. Maybe because they were trying to throw him and Olena off or because they were in a panic and didn't have a clue what to do. Cale voted for the latter. They both looked like scared kids.

As the girl sprinted by him, Cale made a grab for her. But the moment he touched her, a jolt of electricity surged through his fingers, into his hand and up his arm. He instantly released her.

"She shocked me," he said incredulously to Olena.

"I heard she has powerful magic."

"Now you tell me."

"I'll get her."

Olena moved faster than Cale could see. One second she was beside him, and the next she was standing in front of the girl, her hand wrapped around her biceps before she could run out the door.

The girl struggled against Olena's grip. And it looked like Olena was trying not to show how much pain she was in. He could just imagine how much current was going through her.

"Ivy," Olena said. "We just want to talk to you."

"Screw you, cops," she hissed, still trying to get out of Olena's firm hold.

"We're not cops. I'm a crime-scene investigator and this is Agent Braxton from Interpol. We want to talk to you about your uncle Luc."

That stopped her struggle and brought tears to her eyes. "Something's happened, hasn't it?"

Olena nodded, letting go of the girl's arm. "I'm very sorry. Your uncle is dead."

The tears fell freely. "I knew it. I knew it."

"Do you know who killed him, Ivy?" Cale asked. "Anything you can tell us will help."

She glanced from him to Olena and back to him. It looked liked she was searching for the truth in his statement. Looking to see if she could truly trust them.

"I told him it was wrong. I told him they'd find a way to kill him for it."

"Who, Ivy?"

Wringing her hands together, she pursed her lips, then opened her mouth, but she didn't get a chance to say anything before all hell broke loose.

Olena must've sensed something was wrong before Cale did because she grabbed Ivy and wrapped her body around the girl, propelling them both to the floor before two masked gunmen dressed completely in black burst into the makeshift club.

The remaining young people screamed in panic as the assailants opened fire. Cale's first instinct was to aid Olena, even though logic told him the vampire would be all right.

He drew his weapon as he dived to the floor, barely being missed by two bullets that slammed into the wooden post inches from him. He crawled across the floor to one of the torn and frayed sofas and popped back up with his weapon raised.

It was pandemonium in the faintly lit room. Some of the colored lights had been shot out so it was difficult to see much of anything. He knew that the gunmen were still at the front of the place near the exit, but he couldn't pinpoint their exact location, not with some of the young people still staggering around, some shot and bleeding, others in shock.

He glanced behind him and saw Olena still down on the ground. He couldn't see her clearly, but it appeared that she wasn't moving. What if the gunmen were using silver bullets? Would they damage her enough to kill her? He couldn't be sure. He knew vampires could take a lot of damage and that most times the only thing that could kill them was decapitation, fire, or having their hearts ripped out. But a silver bullet to the heart?

The gunmen opened fire again, grazing the room with bullets. They were still at the front of the room. Squinting into the gloom, Cale could make out one shape, holding the distinctive outline of a rifle, near the door. At the lull in gunfire, Cale jumped up, fired three shots in that direction and ran toward Olena's prone form.

He heard a muffled curse from that direction, so he was hoping that meant one of his bullets had hit the target. In a panic to get to Olena, he slid down on his leg alongside her. He grabbed her around the waist to move her.

"Olena."

She grunted in response.

He quickly surveyed her body. There were two holes in the back of her shirt. Blood oozed out of both wounds. His stomach churned over, his heart hammered in his throat. Maybe he was too late. He had to bite down on his lip to calm himself.

"I'm okay. Help me up," she groaned.

"You've been shot."

"I know." She pushed up with her hands, and then looked around. "Where's Ivy?"

"I don't know." With his arm still around her waist, he helped her to her feet. She wobbled once but then stood straight. But he wasn't going to let go of her. He didn't think he could.

More shots were fired in their direction. Firing back, Cale propelled them both across the room. As they neared the far wall, Olena kicked out her leg and made a hole in the wall. They fell through it and into the other room. As they rolled onto the floor together in a heap, Cale could hear sirens in the background. Finally, the cavalry had arrived.

He pushed up into a sitting position. Olena was beside him, her face grimacing in pain. He tore off his jacket, then his shirt and balled it up. Turning her slightly, he pressed the fabric against her wounds.

"I'm fine, Cale, really." She tried to stand up, but he kept her sitting. "We have to find Ivy."

"You've been shot, Olena. You're not fine." He pressed the shirt tighter against her back. "We'll find her after you've been looked at."

"It's just lead. My body will expel the bullets. If it had been silver then I might be in some trouble."

He shook his head in amazement. Most people would've been bleeding to death with two holes in their back, but not his girl. Nope, she was going to pop the bullets out of her body just like that. It was very strange.

And the notion that he was thinking about Olena as being his girl wasn't lost on him, either. He'd been nearly out of his mind when he saw that she'd been shot. Even though deep down he knew because she was a vampire she'd survive, that one moment of pure panic at her eventual death had nearly paralyzed his heart.

Olena turned to smile at him. "Thanks for the first aid. I'm really touched—" Then she paused and her eyes got wide and her mouth gaped open.

She reached for him, her hands scrambling to touch his chest. He grinned, his ego swelling. She was crazy for him. It was a weird time to have sex, but he wasn't going to say no this time. Nope, he wasn't going to say no ever again. He wanted her way too much to deny himself any longer.

"God, Cale. You've been shot."

"What?" He looked down and saw a thick crimson trail down his side along his ribs.

She took the same balled-up shirt he'd used on her, found a clean section and pressed it up under his arm. And when she did that, the pain that had been absent this whole time came hard. In a rush, it swooped over him, making his head spin.

"Shit. I think I'm going to pass out."

She helped him lie down on his back on the floor. "You're going to be all right. The bullet didn't go in. It just grazed you."

He stared up in her eyes and lost himself in them. She was so damn beautiful; it almost hurt to look at her, even with dust and dirt in her hair and dirty streaks across her perfect, pale face.

"I'll only feel better if you kiss me, luv."

Smiling, she leaned down and pressed her lips to his. "There. Is the pain gone?"

"Almost."

She kissed him again. It was deeper and harder. Fierce. He lifted his one arm, buried his hand in her hair and pulled her closer, deepening the kiss. He could drown in her and be perfectly happy.

"Everyone okay over here?" They broke apart just as an EMT with a big bright flashlight knelt down beside Cale. He nodded to Olena. "Hey, Olena."

She returned the greeting. "Trevor." Olena pulled the shirt away from his wound. "The bullet grazed him."

Trevor, the EMT, inspected the wound. His fingers poked and prodded at Cale, but he didn't care. He just kept his attention on Olena. He worried that the pain was making him woozy and giddy because he couldn't seem to tear his gaze away from the vampiress. Maybe it was the fleeting thought of losing her that made him so adamant never to take his eyes off her again. Or it could be he was in serious trouble of losing his heart to her.

Maybe it was a little of both.

"We're going to need to stitch him up. I'll get a stretcher and we'll take him to the hospital."

Cale shook his head. "No hospital. Just stitch me up here."

"It would be better—"

"I'm not going to any damn hospital. I don't need to. Not when there's probably a bunch of kids over there who need it more than I do."

Olena shook her head. "He's a stubborn ass. Just sew him here."

With a sigh, Trevor opened up his bag and took out a large needle and some thread. "It's going to hurt."

"It already hurts, mate. Just get it over with."

After cleaning the wound, Trevor pinched Cale's flesh together and stuck the needle through. Cale had to suck in a breath to stop from screaming out.

Olena patted him on the chest. "I'm going to go check out what happened next door."

"Okay."

She pressed a quick a kiss to his lips, then stood. He watched her as she walked through the hole they'd made and into the other room. It still made his stomach roil to see the bloody holes in her back. At least the bleeding had stopped.

"It's weird, isn't it?"

Cale glanced at the EMT. "What is?"

Trevor nodded toward the hole Olena stepped through. "Seeing how they can heal so fast."

"I take it you're not a vampire."

Trevor shook his head. "Witch. Healing magic."

Cale winced again, as another stitch went in. He'd had stitches before, a couple of knife wounds, one on his leg and the other down his back, but this one was particularly painful. This was actually the first time he'd been shot. And it wasn't very much fun.

"The first time I treated a gunshot wound on a vampire I nearly lost my cool. It was close to the heart and I started CPR."

"What happened?"

"She slapped me across the face and told me to get it together."

Cale sniffed. "Let me guess. Olena?"

Trevor nodded. "Yup. I'd been such a bumbling fool that she grabbed the forceps from my kit and pulled out the bullet herself. She gave it to me." He smiled. "I keep it in my pocket as a reminder."

"Does it ever get easier, seeing that and not being able to do anything about it?"

Trevor shook his head. "Nope. I still panic every time."

Cale sighed. He wasn't sure he could handle seeing Olena hurt like that over and over again, without being able to help. It made him feel weak.

"So, healing magic, huh? Do you have something for the pain, then?"

Trevor nodded. "Of course."

"What? Then why didn't you give it to me?" Cale sputtered.

"Because I thought you wanted to be all tough and cool in front of Olena." Trevor smiled wryly.

"Mate, I'm always tough and cool."

With a laugh, Trevor finished tying off the stitch. After putting away the needle and thread, he took out a small tube of ointment. He squeezed some onto his gloved finger and smoothed it over Cale's side.

The relief was instant and Cale sighed. "That's brilliant. Can I have a tube of that stuff?"

"Yeah, here." Trevor gave him the tube.

"Help me up."

Trevor helped Cale sit up, and Cale slid the tube of magical pain relief into his pants pocket just as Olena came back into the room.

She came up alongside him and offered him her hand. He took it and she pulled him to his feet. "All patched up?"

He twisted his arm, thinking that the pain would zip through him, but it didn't. It was as if he'd never been injured.

Cale smiled. "Yup. Trevor is a miracle worker."

"Good." She smiled in return. But the smile didn't quite reach her eyes.

Trevor packed up his bag and nodded to them both as he went to help his partners in the other room, which Cale assumed was a bloodbath.

"What's the verdict?" Cale asked Olena.

"Two dead. Three wounded. And no Ivy anywhere."

"She must've gotten out," he said as he reached down to grab his jacket and shirt off the floor. His shirt was ruined, so he shoved it into his jacket pocket.

"I called Gabriel and he's put out an APB on her."

"That's good." He went to slip his jacket on, but Olena grabbed it and helped him into it. "Thanks."

"No problem."

"Now what? Back to the lab?"

She wrapped an arm around him. "Back to your hotel."

He smiled. "Olena, luv, you're so forward. I like that in a woman."

"You need rest and food."

"I feel good."

"You won't when that magical ointment wears off."

"What ointment?"

"The one I smell on you. I know Trevor gave you something." She hugged him tighter and walked with him out of the room.

"I guess there isn't too much I could get by you, huh?"

She shook her head, but there was a little smile on her lips. "No. So don't even try."

He sighed. "All right. Take me home then, luv. I'm in no shape to argue."

Chapter 15

When they'd reached Cale's hotel room, Olena had settled him down onto the sofa and then fixed him some herbal tea. What he hadn't known was that she'd added some valerian root, which she'd gotten from one of the other medics. It was a sleeping potion. One that had immediate effects.

Cale hadn't been able to protest by the time it ran through his system and he'd realized what was happening. One minute he was glaring at her and the next he was snoring like a water buffalo.

The man needed some rest. He'd been on the go since arriving in Nouveau Monde and hadn't given himself any kind of break. She wondered if he thought he needed to prove himself above and beyond because, unlike the rest of them, he was human.

She'd put his feet up on the sofa and tucked a pillow under his head, even covered him with a blanket she'd found in the bedroom. He'd be out for about three hours. Enough time to clean herself up and figure out what they were going to do next.

In the bathroom, Olena stripped off her clothes and inspected the wounds in her back. One bullet had gone into her upper left shoulder and the other into her right shoulder blade. Neither injury was of any real consequence. The pain had dulled to a muted throb.

She pressed on the wound in her left shoulder, pushing and prodding at the bullet she could feel just inside her flesh. She would expel it in time, but she decided to hurry it along. Digging her finger in, she fished out the lead and dropped the bloody bullet into the sink.

Next she tried to reach the other hole, but it was in an awkward place and she couldn't quite make it. That bullet would have to come out on its own. Thank goodness she didn't scar. She'd look like a golf ball by now, with all the pitted holes.

She turned on the shower, the hotter the better, and stepped into the hard, scalding spray. Closing her eyes, she let the hot water wash away all the pain and exhaustion she felt. Although it did nothing to the guilt eating away at her.

In her mind she could see the bodies of the dead teens. She knew it wasn't her fault, but she still felt like there should've been something she could have done to prevent it. She'd sensed something off moments before the gunmen appeared. But would it have been enough time to warn anyone?

The only thing Olena had managed to do was hopefully save Ivy's life. At least she thought she had. She remembered tackling the girl to the floor, with her body for protection. The bullet holes in her back attested to that. But then where did the girl disappear to?

As she'd lain on the floor, she'd thought for sure that the girl was still safely under her. She'd lost consciousness for barely a minute. Obviously, that had been enough time for Ivy to push out from under Olena's body and escape. The girl had probably gone to ground. It would be very difficult to find her now. But they had to.

The girl knew who'd killed Luc. She knew

what he'd been messed up in. She knew, and that was probably what had prompted those men to shoot the place apart. Ivy was the key to the whole case.

Wiping the water from her face, Olena shut off the tap and opened the shower door. Eyes still closed, she stepped out into the cool air of the bathroom, reaching for the towel she'd set out for herself on the counter. But it wasn't there.

"Looking for something?"

She peeked one eye open to see Cale, shirtless, leaning against the counter, the towel clutched in his hand. Although his gaze was one of hunger and heat, he didn't look too happy.

"You should still be sleeping."

"You drugged me."

"You needed to rest. If I hadn't, you'd be all gung-ho to do a city-wide search for the girl." She grabbed for the towel but he held it out of her reach. "You would've crashed and burned within hours of that. I need you to be strong. I can't be worrying about you."

His eyes darkened. "You don't think I'm strong enough?"

Suddenly apprehensive, Olena took a step back. He looked really dangerous and unpredictable. A trickle of apprehension laced her system. It wasn't fear necessarily, but she was afraid of what he was going to do.

"I didn't say that, Cale. I think you're plenty strong for—" She stopped.

"For a human?" He dropped the towel and took a step toward her. "Is that what you were going to say?"

She put her hand up to ward him off. She knew that look in his eyes. Heat, hunger, need, anger, fury, all mixed together in an explosive, lethal dose. She didn't know if she'd survive it.

"Cale," she warned.

He didn't heed her. He completely ignored her warning as he breached the distance between them and, grabbing her upper arms, slammed her up against the closed shower door. The impact rattled her a bit. But there was no mistaking the hot ache between her thighs.

With what sounded like a growl deep in his throat, Cale slid his hands down her slick body and wrapped his arms around her derriere. Squeezing her tight, he picked her up, kneed her legs apart and settled himself between them.

"Is that bloody well strong enough for you?"

"Oh, yeah," she breathed, finding it hard to

speak. Desire, hot and hearty, surged through her. Her heart hammered in her chest, eager for what Cale's dark gaze promised.

"I'm not stopping this time." He leaned into her mouth, his lips brushing lightly against hers. "You're going to take everything I give you." Then he kissed her, hard, sweeping his tongue inside her mouth.

She wound her hands in his hair and hung on as he took her mouth, eagerly nipping and biting at her lips and tongue. She returned every nip, every tug with her own. She was ravenous for him. The past two days had been like staring at a buffet table unable to eat, even though pangs of hunger ripped through her belly.

Frantic for him, Olena reached down between them and undid the button and zipper on his pants. Wiggling, Cale managed to squirm out of them and kick them away. She groaned in anticipation at the sight of his erection straining against his white cotton shorts.

When he ground himself against her, she thought she'd come. She was that urgent for him, that hot and wet and open for him. She couldn't wait any longer to have him. It had to be now or she'd go mad.

"Now, Cale. Now. I can't wait any longer."

Though his arms quivered from the strain of holding her up, Cale let go of her with one hand and reached down to pull his shorts off.

Olena hated to see him struggle needlessly. Lifting her arms up, she hooked her hands over the shower door and held herself up. She tightened the hold her legs had around his waist. She could hold herself up there all day if it meant Cale could ravage her with both his hands and his mouth and whatever else he wanted to use. She was his completely and utterly. He could do with her what he wanted. And she'd take pleasure in every single delicious second of it.

Cale could barely breathe with the exhilaration surging through him. Sweat slicked his body. His muscles quivered and shook with anticipation. The urgency of having Olena made him weak-kneed and panting.

With one hand, he tugged at his shorts, desperate to get them off. Once he managed to pull them down his thighs, they dropped to the floor and he stepped out of them. Damn, he was as hard as steel and aching beyond reason. Heat pooled inside him, nearly searing him from the inside out. Only Olena could quench him now.

Only she could slake this aching, burning need that pulsed inside him.

He'd been angry when he'd woken on the sofa, feeling drugged and lethargic. He'd had every intention of reaming her out when he'd entered the bathroom. But when she opened the shower door and stepped out, her whole body slick with water, he stopped. He'd thought her gorgeous before, but he'd never seen a woman as intensely sexy as Olena naked and sopping wet.

He'd gotten hard instantly. And since then he'd just gotten harder. He hadn't known that was possible. He wanted her so much it hurt. A fierce, frantic ache thumped inside him, and the only thing he could think of to satisfy that, to end his suffering, was to plunge himself deep inside her beautiful body.

Her eyes were as deep as the ocean as he nuzzled his hardness against her hot core. Her lips parted and she gasped. The sight of her chewing on her bottom lip nearly did him in. The tips of her fangs worried her skin. With her arms up and pressed against the shower door, her breasts pushed out toward him, perfect and pale, with rosy, puckered nipples. It was an invitation he couldn't refuse.

"Bloody hell, Olena, I can't hold on."

"Then don't."

He took himself in hand and stroked himself up and down the slick warmth of her. Groaning low in his throat, he thrust into her, hard and fast.

"Ah," she cried out as she moved against him.

Leaning down, he sucked one beautiful nipple into his mouth. As he suckled on her, he rocked his pelvis, gaining a rhythm.

"Yes," she moaned as she ground her sex against his every time he moved.

He increased his rhythm. Gripping her tight, he pounded into her again and again. Sweat dripped off his forehead and dotted her still-wet body. Clamping his eyes shut, he buried his face in the crook of her neck and concentrated on thrusting. In and out. Long and hard. He kept working and thrusting until he couldn't think any longer.

Everything became one hot rush of pure pleasure. Thrusting hard and fast, Cale squeezed Olena tight. He was losing his mind. He was losing his breath. Everything was light and dark and hot and cold. He couldn't reason beyond it. Sensations he'd never experienced before surged through him in one fierce blast. With one last thrust he buried himself deep, and like an explosion of sound and color and emotion, he came in a brutal flood.

"Olena," he cried, clamping his eyes tight against the rush of emotions drowning him.

With a long, low groan, she fell forward and wrapped her arms around his head, stroking her fingers through his hair. He felt her lips on his cheek, kissing his sweat away.

His legs and arms were shaking. He didn't know how long he could stay on his feet. Picking her up, he carried her over to the bathroom counter and set her down. They had still been joined when he moved her, but he slipped out of her when she leaned back against the fogged mirror.

She looked at him with a wry tilt to her mouth. He stared at her, unsure of what to say. Then she smiled, and her whole face lit up with a warm glow. It was the loveliest moment he'd ever witnessed.

"I think I can safely declare you completely healed," she said still breathing hard.

He laughed, and leaned down and rested his head against hers. "I don't know about that. I don't think I can move anymore."

Laughing with him, she wrapped her arms

around him and nuzzled her face into his chest. "Me, either."

He ran his hands over her damp hair and kissed the top of her head. He could stay in this position forever and not want for anything. Well, maybe food. His stomach decided to agree with him and grumbled quite loudly.

That made Olena laugh even more. "I guess that's the cue that we need to take this into the living room and order room service."

"Agreed." He took a step back, feeling both languid and light-headed. "But you're going to have to walk on your own. I'm not sure I can even carry myself."

She slid off the counter and grabbed his hand in hers. "That's all right. You've already proven to me how strong you are. I don't think I can stand another demonstration. I'm way too sore."

With Olena in the crook of his arm, they walked side by side, naked and sweaty, into the living room to eat. For now they had both sated their other hunger.

Chapter 16

Olena had ordered pretty much one of everything on the room-service menu. She wasn't sure what Cale wanted; besides, she was hungry enough to eat most of it if he didn't want it. That was one of the best things about being a vampire—eating ten thousand calories and not gaining an ounce. Besides that, she loved the taste of food. It was a pleasure to eat.

She'd also gone out to the vending machine in the hallway and bought two bottles of AB positive. Their little tryst had worn her completely out, plus she had to replenish the blood she'd lost from being shot.

Cale didn't say much as they ate. But he did watch her. Probably because he couldn't believe she could eat so much and stay so svelte.

They'd also finally managed to put some clothes back on after realizing that eating naked likely wasn't the best idea. Not if they truly wanted to eat and not end up in each other's arms again. Cale was incredibly attractive with clothes on. Naked, he was downright impossible to resist.

Cale dressed again in his usual manner, dress pants and shirt and tie. Because her shirt had been ruined, she borrowed one of his. Although it was a clean, crisp shirt, it still smelled like Cale. Olena had to fight the urge to bury her nose into the collar and sniff.

After taking one last bite of the delicious prime rib, Olena set down her fork and leaned back in her chair, officially declaring herself done.

Cale shook his head. "Are all your appetites this ferocious?"

"Oh, yeah."

His lips twitched up into a lopsided grin. "Lucky me."

"Hmm, we'll see about that, fella." She liked

that even now there was this sexual tension between them, this flirtation. She didn't ever want to lose that.

Picking up his coffee cup, he sat back in his chair and took a sip. He sighed. "So, this Ivy, I think she's at the root of all this."

"I do, too. She knows something. Something worth killing for."

"Any ideas on how to track her down?"

"I don't know, other than just hitting the downtown streets. There are a lot of places to hide in Nouveau Monde."

"Yeah, but she's got to come up for air sometime. She's a witch, right? Doesn't she have to stock up on materials?"

Olena laughed. "She's a dhampir. Half vampire, half witch. And no, I don't think she uses potions and spells. I think her power lies within her. She was sparking something fierce when I grabbed her. She gave me a major jolt of electricity."

He flexed his hand as if remembering the pain she was sure he'd felt when he'd touched her. "Is that what that was? I've never experienced anything like that before."

"It's a rare gift. If she can harness energy like that, she is indeed a very powerful witch."

"Do you think that's what they're after?"

"Her power?"

He nodded.

"I never thought of that. But in what way? It's not like she was in the safety-deposit box."

Cale leaned forward in his chair and rubbed a hand over his face and through his hair. "Maybe she made something with that kind of power. Like an amulet or charm."

Olena considered that for a moment. She knew some witches who were incredibly powerful but mostly used their gifts for good and healing. She'd heard of some who could harness the elements but only to a small degree. Not anything of consequence. Nothing that she thought could be used in any major way. But she wasn't an expert on witches.

She grabbed her purse and rummaged through it for her cell phone.

"Who are you calling?"

"François, at the lab. He's a witch and would know more about this than I do. Maybe he can shed some light on the powers Ivy seems to possess."

The phone rang twice before a very suave French voice answered. *"Bonjour, mon amour."*

"*Bonjour,* François."

She'd dated the witch a couple of times. It was nothing serious. Just a couple of fun nights out. He was too young for her in many ways, both in age and life experience. But he'd been a nice distraction when she needed it. He'd known going in that nothing would develop between them. But he still liked to flirt. She let him. After all, it was always good to practice.

"What can I do for the lovely Olena today?"

"I have some questions about a dhampir who's of interest in the case I'm working on. I'm going to put you on speaker, okay? So Agent Braxton can hear as well."

"*D'accord.* Is he attractive?"

She shook her head. "Behave."

"Sure, whatever."

Olena pressed a button on her phone, and then set it down on the table between herself and Cale.

"Can you hear me, François?"

"*Oui, mon amour.* Ask away."

Cale bristled a little at his comment but sat forward, his elbows on his knees.

"Have you ever heard of a witch being able to control electricity?"

"Hmm, control it, no. Mess around with it, yes."

"What do you mean, 'mess around'?" Cale asked.

"Some witches have problems around electrical things. Their auras can interfere with the power. So the lights could go out, or appliances might not work around them. Cell phones buzz out."

"Could the fact that this girl is half vampire make a difference with her magical ability?" Olena asked.

"Maybe. It depends on how powerful her magical parent and her vampire parent are. I can't tell you for sure without knowing these things."

"This girl gave us a major electrical shock just by touching us," Olena said. "It seemed like a defense mechanism."

"Hmm, that's cool."

She smiled at his cavalier attitude. He worked hard at his job, but everything else just slid off him, as if he didn't care. But Olena knew that he did.

Cale inched forward a little more in his seat. "Let's say she has this gift. Could she create something powerful with it? A weapon of some kind, maybe?"

Olena looked at him. He had something in

mind. Something he hadn't shared with her. Maybe it was a hunch or maybe it was more, and he'd just decided to leave her out of it. It put her back up.

"A weapon?" François whistled. "Like a bomb or something?"

"Yes, like a bomb."

Olena shifted in her chair. "Is there something you're not telling me, Cale?"

He didn't meet her gaze. "Not really."

"Not really?"

"Are you two arguing?" François asked. "You better be nice to my girl, Agent Braxton."

"Your girl?" Cale guffawed.

"Yes, my girl. She's—"

"François, don't start trouble, please."

"But, Olena, *mon amour,* he sounds too gruff for you."

Olena tried not to scream. "François, could you please answer the question?" She could hear his long, drawn-out sigh and she shook her head.

"Yes, I suppose. It would be just like making witchlight, or a fireball. We contain the element inside a type of force field, a containment unit type of thing. If this witch can harness electricity or other harmful power, in theory, she could produce an explosive device."

Cale sat back on the sofa, as if satisfied that his theory had been proven right.

"Thank you, François."

"You are very welcome, Olena, my lovely. When are you coming back to the lab? I miss seeing your beautiful face."

Olena grabbed the phone before François could say any more potentially problematic things. "I will see you soon." She quickly flipped the phone closed and set it back onto the table.

"Is there something you want to share with me? Some theory you have?"

Cale crossed his arms over his chest. "Are you dating this guy?"

"What? No. I'm not dating François."

"It sure sounded as if there's something between the two of you."

Olena stood and walked the room, agitated. "He was just trying to rile you up. Which obviously worked. I didn't realize you were the jealous type."

"I'm not," he scoffed.

"You could've fooled me." She stopped in front of him. "And besides, what does it matter? You'll be leaving after the case. And we aren't involved. We had sex." She turned to look at him, her hands on her hips. "Good sex, but that's all."

He stood before her. "Is that all it was? Just sex?"

"Of course. What else is there?"

"Okay," he said flippantly, then turned to go into the bedroom.

She followed him. "What do you mean by 'okay'?"

He went into the closet and pulled a jacket from a hanger. "I mean okay. It's just sex and nothing more." He slid his jacket on.

She eyed him. Was that hurt she saw in his gaze? Did he want more from her than just sex? "Right. Nothing more. It would just complicate our working relationship, anyway."

"You said earlier that it wouldn't complicate things for you."

She shook her head. "No, I said sex wouldn't complicate things for me. That other stuff? Big complications."

"Right." He grabbed his BlackBerry and slid it into his inside jacket pocket. "Let's get to work. We need to track down this girl." He walked out of the bedroom.

Olena followed him out. "Speaking of the girl, why would you think that she could create a bomb? What aren't you telling me?"

"Before I came here I was working on another case dealing with terrorists. I got a vision of the bank explosion and vampire faces when I touched some wires from another bomb. That's why I'm here. I think there may be terrorists involved."

"Vampire terrorists?"

He looked at her, an eyebrow arched. "What, you don't think that's possible?"

"I just never considered it before."

"Humans don't corner the market on terror." He walked toward the door and opened it. "Shall we?"

She grabbed her purse but paused before exiting. "Are we okay? I don't want any difficulties between us."

"We're fine, Olena. We had sex, it was good, and now we're going back to work. No problems."

She nodded and left the room, but somehow she didn't believe him. There definitely was a problem. What she couldn't decide was if that was a good thing or a bad thing.

Chapter 17

For three hours Cale and Olena canvassed the downtown streets looking for Ivy Seaborn. They went from comic-book stores to cafés to alternative nightclubs. So far, no one had known who she was or had seen her around. Either the girl was a ghost or someone was lying.

Cale went with lying. No one could disappear that effectively. There was always a trace left behind. Always.

He and Olena hadn't talked much since leaving his hotel and walking the streets. He wasn't sure what he wanted to say, if anything. She'd made it clear to him that it had been all about sex and nothing more. During a different time in his life with a different woman, that might have sat well with him. But not with Olena. He was coming to realize that he wanted more than just the amazing, hot, sweaty sex they'd just had. He wanted to know her. He wanted to know something about her that no one else in the world knew. Some secret that she carried inside. He wanted that to be his and his only, so that no matter where he went or what happened to him in the future, he would always have that little piece of her with him.

It was a corny notion, but he couldn't seem to extract it from his head or his heart. It was strange for him to feel this way about a vampiress. But he did. And he wasn't exactly sure what he wanted to do about it.

After hitting yet another small café, they decided to stop and grab a coffee for themselves and sit for a few minutes at one of the street-side tables. It seemed the perfect way to watch the waning sun.

Sipping his drink, Cale glanced at her. "How long have you been an investigator?"

She looked at him, seemingly surprised by the

question. "About ten years. You? How long with Interpol?"

"Six years. I was an inspector for Scotland Yard before that."

"Did you always want to be in law enforcement?"

He nodded. "Yeah. My dad was an officer. I grew up around it my whole life." He smiled, remembering something from his past. "I tried a stint in crime, but it didn't last long. My dad found out and beat the tar out of me. I think I was in that gang for a whole two weeks."

Olena smiled and sipped her coffee.

"What about you?" he asked her. "Did you always want to be an investigator?"

She set her cup down and leaned forward on the table. "No. I grew up wanting to be free from my duty as a servant. I wanted to marry well. I wanted to be a stage actress. I wanted to serve my country in a time of war." She smiled wistfully. "That's the funny thing about living almost three hundred years—you can want and get to do many things. I did all of those things and more. Now I want to make a difference in other people's lives. So this is what I've chosen to do with these years. Maybe in twenty years I'll feel differently."

He watched her with curiosity. He'd known she was old for a vampire but had no idea she'd been around that long. He marveled at all the things, good and bad, that she must've seen and experienced. It was amazing to him. And strange.

"You were married before?"

"Several times." She met his gaze. It was as if she was daring him to say something about it.

He sat back and contemplated that. He knew it was ridiculous to think that she'd be chaste or had never experienced true love. He was closing in on forty and he'd had his fair share of lovers over the years. He didn't even want to think how many it had been for Olena.

But the notion that she'd been in love before and had devoted her life, or at least a portion of it, to another man made his gut clench and set his teeth on edge.

"Does it bother you that I've been married before?"

He pulled a face. "No, why would it?"

"Well, you seem a little agitated about it."

"I'm not. I was just making conversation." He grabbed his coffee and took a sip and eyed her over the rim. "How many times is several?"

"Four."

"There's no bitter ex-husband in the background, is there? Should I be worried about an angry, jealous vampire coming after me?" He meant it as a good-humored joke to lighten the mood, but the look that crossed her face told him there was no humor in her reaction.

"I'm four times widowed, so I don't think you'll have to worry." She stood and tossed her empty Styrofoam cup into the trash can. "Let's get back to the canvassing."

Cale stood and had to rush a little to catch up with her. He touched her arm to stop her. "I didn't mean to hit a sore spot."

She looked at him and smiled a little. "You didn't. Not really. It's just sometimes it hits me, and I realize how alone I really am and will be for a long, long time."

He wanted to hug her then. Wrap her in his arms and press his lips to her temple and breathe her in. He ached to take her pain away. It was strange that this woman, this Otherworld being, who didn't need anyone or anything to protect her because of her superpowered genetics, was the one person he longed to shield from all the world's harm. She really brought out his protective instinct.

Although he wanted desperately to soothe her, he didn't think she'd appreciate it. She was a woman innately proud of her independence. She was strong both inside and out, and he didn't want to seem as if he was belittling that. He wished she could understand that it was those qualities that drew him to her so fiercely.

He smiled. "Well, you're not alone right now. You have me to order around, if you want."

That made her laugh. "Thanks, Cale. So generous of you to offer."

He laughed with her. "Hey, I'm not just a pretty face. I have a great personality, too."

Her eyebrow rose. And it was so sexy, he nearly groaned. "I've noticed."

He was in grave danger of leaning in to kiss her. He didn't much care that they were out on the street, on the job. His lips wanted to be on hers right now. By the way she was looking at him, he suspected that she wouldn't have minded one bit.

He took a step closer to her, indicating his intentions. She raised her head just a little to let him in. Except her gaze passed over his shoulder and her eyes widened. "She's right across the street."

"What?" He was about to turn his head when Olena put her hand on his chin to stop him.

"Don't turn around. You'll spook her. So far I don't think she's noticed us."

"What's she doing?"

Olena nestled into him and put her arms around his neck. She settled her head onto his shoulder so she could watch the girl. "She's standing in front of a grocery store. There's an apple cart behind her. It looks like she's getting ready to steal a few."

"She must be hungry. Do you think she's been living on the street?"

"Maybe. Moving around so no one can find her."

Although they were doing their job, Cale liked how close Olena was. His body couldn't stop from responding to her. Like a moth to a flame, he was drawn to her.

He moved his hands up and down her back and nuzzled his face into her hair. "How do you want to play it?"

"I'm fast. She won't be able to outrun me."

"I could distract her and you could take her by surprise."

"Okay." She moved back, dropping her arms from his shoulders. He felt the loss of her heat instantly. "You go that way down the street. Make sure she sees you."

Cale had no doubt that Ivy would see him. He was probably one of the only men in the area in a suit.

They split apart and Cale started down the street the way Olena had indicated. He walked quickly with his eyes on Ivy the whole time. It took maybe two minutes for the girl to spot him, and only a second for her to panic and run.

But Olena was there in a flash, effectively blocking Ivy. The girl looked around in alarm, searching for a way out, but she was kidding herself if she thought she could outmaneuver Olena again.

Cale jogged across the street toward them. When he got there, Olena had Ivy by the arm and was trying to reason with her.

"We can protect you, Ivy."

The girl was crying. "No, you can't. No one can. They killed Uncle Luc and he was powerful. They'll find me and kill me, too."

"Who are they?" Cale asked.

Instead of answering, she shook her head and cried harder. Olena pulled Ivy closer and wrapped an arm around her. "Let's get you to a safe place. We'll order in some food and we can talk." The girl just clung to Olena's arm.

As they walked to Olena's vehicle, Cale realized that finding Ivy had been the easy part. Getting her to talk was going to be difficult.

Ivy Seaborn was the key to the whole case, but Cale had no idea how to unlock her secrets.

Chapter 18

About an hour later, after convincing Gabriel to give her the okay, Olena had managed to secure a safe house in which to stash Ivy. At first the girl didn't want to go, but Olena assured her that no one other than a few people on the crime-scene team knew about the house and Ivy's involvement.

After she managed to get the girl settled into the small second-floor apartment, Olena ordered takeout for everyone. Everyone included her, Ivy and Cale. For now, anyway. Eventually a second team would arrive to relieve Olena and Cale.

But for now they were just like a family, sitting at the kitchen table and munching on spring rolls, chow mein and kung pao chicken.

Ivy gobbled it all up like she hadn't eaten in a week. By the looks of her stringy white-blond hair and the sweat stains on her dingy gray T-shirt, she hadn't showered in that long, either.

Cale sat silently eating and carefully watching both Olena and Ivy. She wondered if he was giving her the lead on questioning the girl. It seemed that way. Ivy had looked at him a few times, warily but with a bit of curiosity thrown in. Or it could've been she found Cale attractive. Olena wouldn't blame the girl for crushing on him. He was definitely a looker.

When Ivy looked like she was slowing down a bit, Olena made her move.

"This chicken is pretty good," she said, starting off slow and easy.

Ivy shrugged. "It's okay."

Olena looked in the white cardboard container. "There's more here if you want it. Don't want it to go to waste." She slid it over toward Ivy, who emptied the contents onto her plate.

"How long has it been since you've had a decent meal?"

She shrugged again. "I don't know, four or five days."

"Where have you been staying?"

"Here and there. Nowhere for too long." She shoveled the rest of the chicken into her mouth.

Olena glanced at Cale. He was done eating and was now sitting back in his chair watching and waiting. He nodded to her.

Olena leaned forward on the table, her hands out palms down. "I'm sorry about your uncle."

Ivy hesitated, visibly shaken. She set her fork down on her plate. Her head stayed down, as if she was looking at something in her lap.

"Were you close to him?"

Ivy nodded. "He was the only family I had left."

"We want to find those responsible for his death, Ivy. Can you help us with that?"

She didn't respond, but kept staring down.

"These people are bad, Ivy. I believe they are involved in something even bigger. That's why Agent Braxton is here. Something even worse is going to happen. We need your help. You're the only person who can."

Her head came up a little at that.

"We won't be able to find and punish the murderers without you."

She looked up and met Olena's gaze. "I want to help, but I'm afraid."

Olena reached across the table and took Ivy's hand. She wasn't sure if she should make a personal connection with the girl, but she looked so lost and frightened that Olena couldn't help it. A long time ago she'd come to terms with the fact that she'd never have children, so seeing this child suffer needlessly broke Olena's heart.

"I know you're afraid. But we won't let anything happen to you, Ivy. You can trust us."

The girl slowly slid her hand out from under Olena's. She looked from her to Cale and back to her again. "I'm tired. Is there somewhere I can crash?"

Disappointed, Olena nodded. She pointed to an open doorway past the kitchen. "There's a bed in that room with a pillow and blankets. It should be comfy enough."

Ivy stood, pushing her chair back. "I'm sure it beats the cement slab I slept on last night." Without another word, she padded out of the kitchen and into the bedroom. She shut the door behind her.

When she was gone, Olena sighed and looked at Cale. "This is going to be a lot harder than I thought."

"She's obviously been through a lot and isn't the trusting sort," Cale said.

"She has info we need. How do we get it?"

Cale frowned. "I don't know. I'm not skilled with dealing with kids."

"Me, either. I'm not sure I even was one."

Cale laughed.

Olena stood and started to clean off the table.

"So I guess we're the babysitters," Cale said, nodding toward the closed bedroom door.

She leaned on the counter. "Yeah. She's the best lead we have right now, so I guess we're stuck for a while."

As Cale pushed away from the table, he started to roll up his shirtsleeves. "I'll wash, you dry."

Olena laughed as he sidled up to the counter and turned on the tap to fill the sink. Amused, she watched as he searched in the cupboard under the sink for the dish soap, then dripped some into the hot water.

"Are you getting a kick out of this?" he asked with a twinkle in his eye. He was just as amused at the situation as she was.

"Most definitely."

Olena's heart lightened a little as she and Cale washed and dried the dishes. It was an everyday, mundane act, but with Cale at her side it seemed to transcend that. It made her feel something different, something more about him and about them together. She could picture doing this with him every day. Making dinner, eating it at a small table for two, talking and laughing together, washing up afterward to then take their evening into the living room. She could picture it in her mind and it made her ache all over. It was funny to her that the most unsexual act between them could be the most pivotal.

When he handed her the last plate, his fingers brushed hers. It was enough of a jolt to make her nearly drop the plate. Cale must've noticed, because he was staring at her, at her mouth in particular. It made her burn in all the hard-to-reach places. Places she was hoping he'd touch again soon. Memories of their tryst in his hotel bathroom popped into her mind and she had to swallow the saliva pooling in her mouth.

"I had no idea that washing dishes could be a big turn-on."

Olena laughed. "Me, either."

Cale leaned closer to her, his soapy hands reaching for her. She didn't pull away; she couldn't. His mouth inched toward hers. She parted her lips on a sigh, in anticipation of his kiss.

That was when they heard the noise from the other room.

Cale's head came up. "What the bloody hell was that?"

Olena was already on her way to the bedroom door. "The window. She's gone out the window." She reached for the doorknob.

When her hand wrapped around the metal, she got a jolt of electricity. It pushed her back a couple of feet and she stumbled into Cale. He grabbed her upper arms and kept her steady and on her feet.

"Damn that girl," Olena said.

"Why is she fighting us on this?"

"I don't know. But I've had just about enough." Olena moved toward the door again, her hands clenched at her sides. This time she used her foot on the door and kicked it with all her strength. Splintering along the frame, the door fell like a cut-down tree. Olena rushed into the room.

The room was empty. The multicolored curtains fluttered in the slight breeze blowing in from the open window.

"I thought the window was locked," Cale said as he examined it.

"It was. She's obviously more gifted in magic than we thought. A lock is nothing to a witch with skills."

Cale turned from the window. "Now what?"

Olena spied something on the floor near the bed. She bent down to pick it up. It was a silver bracelet. Though it burned her fingers, she held on to it.

"Looks like Ivy forgot something." She tossed it to Cale. "Think you can get something from it."

Cale examined it in his hand. "I might."

Another sound turned Olena around. It was coming from the front door. "Now what?" She started back toward the kitchen.

"What is it?" Cale followed her into the living area.

"Something…"

Cale must've sensed it just as she did, because he jumped toward her. "Get down!" he yelled. His weight took them both down to the floor.

The front door burst apart and two metal canisters were lobbed into the room through the hole in the wood. Smoke seeped out of them.

"Gas," she said.

"Damn it," Cale murmured in her ear. "Cover your face. We need to get out of here."

Together, they crawled out of the living room. By the time they made it into the kitchen, there were voices coming from the ruined front door.

"Find the girl."

"What about the vampire and the human?"

"Kill them. They're of no further use."

The smoke was filling the apartment quickly. Olena's vision was blurry and her tongue felt thick in her mouth, like she'd eaten too much peanut butter. She glanced at Cale. He obviously wasn't faring any better. He was shaking his head as if trying to clear it.

Olena patted him on the shoulder and pointed to the bedroom.

He shook his head. "We'll be trapped."

"I'll get us out of here."

They crawled to the bedroom, over the busted-down door and to the open window. Olena stood and grabbed the blanket off the bed. She wrapped her hands in the fabric and ran for the window.

"Out we go," Olena said.

Cale didn't hesitate as two masked gunmen with gas masks entered the room, weapons poised. Using his hands, he sprang through the open window, reaching for the fire escape as he did.

Olena didn't even bother.

She jumped through the opening and wrapped her arm around Cale, taking them both down to the ground two stories below.

"Jesus Christ, woman!" he yelled.

In midair, she spun them around so he was on top.

They landed with a thud on the cool, hard cement. Olena felt a rib or two break from the impact. Cale grunted when they hit. Although she'd taken most of the blow, she knew he must've felt something.

Groaning, he rolled off her and onto his back. "You've got to be kidding me. You did not just do that."

"Had to." She tried to roll over onto her side, but the pain ripped through her. Her back was bleeding again. She could tell by the warm stickiness of the shirt she was wearing.

Cale looked over at her. "You're hurt again."

"Nothing that won't heal in a few hours."

He sat up and shook his head. "I'm not sure I can handle watching you get hurt again and again." He winced, and she knew his bullet wound had likely opened up.

"I know it's hard, Cale, but I'll heal. You have to keep reminding yourself of that."

"Yeah." He looked down at his hands. They were rubbed raw and spotted with blood.

Olena tried again to move. This time she was able to sit up, groaning all the way. "Damn, you're heavy." Wincing, she put a hand to her side. "Remind me not to do that again."

"Deal." He stood and then reached down to help her up, which she could tell caused him pain.

Once they were both standing, they hobbled down the alleyway leaning on each other. Sirens could be heard in the background.

As they stepped out of the alley, a police car and an ambulance pulled up to the curb. Another unmarked car zoomed up onto the sidewalk. The driver's door opened and Gabriel jumped out. Once he saw them, he made a beeline for them, ignoring the shouts from officers and EMTs.

"Are you all right?" he asked them.

Olena nodded. "A broken rib or two. Nothing major." She nodded toward Cale. "Cale's hands need bandaging, though."

Gabriel swirled around and shouted for a paramedic. One came running toward them. It was Trevor.

"You two again?" He smiled and was already opening up his kit.

As he went to work on Cale's hands, Olena filled Gabriel in on what had happened.

"How did they find you?" he asked.

That was the million-dollar question. "I don't know. The girl maybe. Somehow they're tracking her."

Gabriel shook his head. "If that was true they would've picked her up on her own without the hassle of taking you two out."

Cale's head came up at that. "One of us is being traced, then."

Olena closed her eyes and shook her head. "Son of a bitch."

"I take it you're the one being tracked." Gabriel eyed Olena.

"Valentino."

Cale cursed.

"He came to my place to give me that information about Ivy. It was a setup. He must've planted something on me."

"We'll take you to the lab and get you examined. If it's electrical, we'll track it down. If it's a magical trace, François will find it."

Olena nodded. She felt like an idiot. She should've realized that Valentino had had an ulterior motive for visiting her. She should've sensed it from him. But the witch had been skilled in charm. Most likely he'd enchanted himself to others. This meant she saw only what he wanted her to see. But still, guilt swirled in her belly. If she'd known, if she'd suspected, those kids in that club wouldn't have been gunned down and she wouldn't have risked Cale's life twice.

That was something she wasn't sure she knew how to deal with.

Chapter 19

Once they were patched up, Gabriel ferried both Cale and Olena back to the lab. They had an officer drive Olena's vehicle back. On the way, the inspector made a call to have someone go over to Valentino's place of residence to pick him up.

At the lab, they were immediately ushered into one of the investigator rooms where François would check them out. Cale didn't know what to think of the young witch investigator who walked in rubbing his hands together gleefully at the prospect of examining Olena for magical tracing spells. After hearing the witch's voice on the phone, Cale didn't expect a lean man with long black hair and downright pretty facial features.

He was surprised that Olena would've dated a man like him. He seemed too young, and too perfect-looking with his sharp cheekbones and smooth, pale skin. He reminded Cale of one of those male models plastered on billboards selling cologne or Calvin Klein underwear.

François's eyes almost lit up at the prospect of being so close to Olena. Cale couldn't blame him really. But it still put his back up. Jealousy boiled inside his gut like acid. The thought of this guy putting his hands on his girl made Cale twitchy. Very twitchy.

"I'm going to need you to take your clothes off, Olena."

"What?" Cale and Olena spoke in unison.

Gabriel put his hand out to stop the protests. "Can you explain please, François?"

François harrumphed. "The spell isn't going to be on your clothes," he explained. "It's going to be on your skin."

"Makes sense," Olena said reluctantly.

Cale totally understood now why the witch was so happy about this. He was going to get to see the vampiress of his dreams in her underwear.

His blood was starting to boil and he had to bite down on his lip to stop himself from telling François to go to hell.

"All right, let's just get this over with." Olena started to unbutton her shirt.

Both François and Gabriel looked over at Cale. François put his hand on his hip. "Maybe you should leave, Agent Braxton."

"Like hell."

"It's okay. He can stay."

Now both François and Gabriel looked at her. She didn't meet either of their gazes.

"Olena," Gabriel started.

"I'm a big girl, thank you, Gabriel. I don't need a lecture."

The inspector looked from her to Cale. There was something in his eyes that Cale couldn't register. Gabriel was definitely measuring him. That he could see. It might've been a lycan thing. He knew that lycans were extremely territorial, and he imagined that the inspector considered Olena his territory. Despite her being of a different species, she was part of his team.

He wondered if Gabriel was going to give him a problem now that he knew Olena's and his relationship had evolved into something else. He hoped not, because Cale had no idea how to handle it. Nor did he know how to handle the relationship. Despite what Olena wanted to believe, it had gone beyond sex. Into what, he had no idea. But he did know that he would fight for it. Fight for them. Even if he had to go toe to toe with an angry lycan.

In the end, Gabriel backed down. "I'm going to step out. You don't need me hovering." He walked out, shutting the door behind him.

Once he was gone, Olena shed her shirt and then started to unbutton her pants. Cale tried not to stare at her, but it proved difficult when she looked like a warrior goddess standing there in her black lace bra. Her sable hair swirled around her like dark silk, and her skin had a slight golden glow. She was mesmerizing.

François, on the other hand, had no qualms about staring at her. It made Cale's gut clench again. He ground his teeth as he watched the young witch gobble up Olena's body with his intense gaze. The urge to walk across the room and squish the little man surged through him. It took all he had to stay glued to the spot.

Olena took off her pants, folded them and set them on the table next to her folded shirt. Cale nearly swallowed his tongue. She was wearing matching black lace panties. He'd seen her naked, had her on the bathroom counter, but seeing her like this, scantily clad and a bit vulnerable, sent his libido into overdrive.

"Okay," she said. "Now what?"

"I need to feel your aura, so can you stand still with your arms out to the side?"

Feel your aura. Cale thought that was the cheesiest line he'd ever heard. He imagined François wanted to feel more than that. But he bit his tongue.

Olena stuck her arms out to the side. As she stood there like a cross, she avoided Cale's gaze. He could imagine how she was feeling right about now. Maybe he was making it worse by being in the room, but he couldn't push himself to leave.

Rubbing his hands together, François neared her. "Just stay still." He raised his hands and set them around her, starting at her head. His hands hovered in the air, mere inches from her. After taking in a deep breath, he started to move them down and around her body.

Cale watched him work, aware that his own body was shaking. He'd had no idea that he could feel this way about someone. He wasn't normally a jealous guy, but watching the witch almost touch Olena on her shoulders, on her arms, on her breasts, was driving him insane.

Olena's gaze met his over top of François's head. By the look in her eyes, he knew she was completely aware of his barely reined-in control. And was not happy about it.

"Can you hurry this up, François?"

"No, I can't. I don't want to miss it because you're pushing me."

He went to his knees then, his hands skimming the slope of Olena's belly and the rise of her hip. His face was just below the rise of her breasts. From François's position, Cale knew his breath would be blowing on her skin. He'd be able to smell her intoxicating scent.

That should've been him on his knees in front of her, worshipping her, not François. The young boy had no business touching her beautiful supple flesh.

He couldn't take it anymore. Clenching his hands, he took a step forward.

"Don't you dare," Olena warned. "Stay right where you are."

Cale stopped in midstride.

"Aha," François declared, "I found it."

Olena glanced down. François had his hands circling her ankles. “Where was it?”

“On the top of your feet.”

“How did a spell get there?” Cale asked, his interest getting the better of him as he breached the rest of the distance to glance down at Olena’s feet.

François shrugged. “He could’ve dripped an ointment onto her skin. Or he could’ve touched her there and planted the spell.”

“He dropped something when he was in my apartment.” Olena shook her head. “I didn’t even think to watch as he picked it up. I had just come out of the shower and had bare feet. He could’ve done it while he crouched down. I was still wet, so I wouldn’t have felt anything if he flicked something onto my skin.”

“Yeah, but I thought spells could be washed off?” Cale was thinking of the sex spell and how he’d showered it off. And he was also thinking about finding Olena in the shower in his hotel room. She was hot and wet when she’d come out.

He had to shake that image away, or he knew he’d get hard thinking about it again.

“Technically, most can be. But this one actually soaked into Olena’s skin.”

"Can you get rid of it?" she asked.

Nodding his head, he stood. "But it will take me some time to conjure an antidotal spell."

"How much time?" Olena asked.

"Three or four hours maximum." François rubbed his hands together again.

Olena picked up her clothes and started to get dressed. "Thank you, François."

He bowed a little to her. "My pleasure, *mon amour.*"

"Yeah, I bet it was," Cale mumbled under his breath.

François glanced at him, a sly little smile on his face. "You seem a little uptight, Agent Braxton. Maybe you should take some time off. Get some sleep. I know it can be difficult for a human to keep up with our pace here in Nouveau Monde." His gaze flicked over to Olena, then back again. "Otherworlders just have a lot more stamina."

"My stamina is fine."

Olena finished buttoning up her shirt. "I'll be back to see you in about three hours, François." She marched over to Cale and grabbed his arm, steering him toward the door.

"I'll be looking forward to it."

Olena pulled him out of the room before he could say anything else.

"What's wrong with you?" she asked him as they walked down the hallway.

"I didn't like the way he was ogling you."

"Ogling me?" She frowned at him. "François doesn't ogle. He's a professional. Unlike some people."

"I am a professional."

She smirked. "Yeah, right. And I bet you're not hard right now." Her gaze dropped to the crotch of his pants. Which of course was an unfair maneuver. Of course he was going to react when she looked at him with her smoldering, sexy gaze.

"You were in your underwear."

She shook her head. "And seeing a woman in her underwear is enough to give you an erection? You're like a damn teenager."

He grabbed her arm and stopped her from walking. He took a step forward, crowding her against the wall. "*You* were in your underwear. *You.* Not some other woman that I don't give a damn about."

"Oh." Her breathing changed then. He could hear it. Her eyes darkened as well. She was acutely aware of his presence. He wondered if she could smell his arousal.

He wanted to kiss her. He wanted to press her up against the wall and take her mouth and her body.

"Cale," she warned, and took a step backward. Her back bumped up into the wall. "This is not the place."

Several technicians passed them in the hall. More than one set of eyes widened at their position.

"Then we'd better find a place," he growled, "because I'm about two minutes away from letting everyone in this lab know how much I want you."

"Your hotel is closer than my place," she said lowly.

"Fine. Let's go."

He took her by the hand and led her down the hallway toward the main lobby.

They ran into Gabriel along the way. His eyebrows shot up as they neared. "We're taking a couple of hours," Cale grunted as they passed right by him.

Gabriel didn't even have a chance to respond before Cale pulled her out the main door.

Chapter 20

The drive to the hotel took exactly six minutes and forty-five seconds, according to Olena's watch. She sped the entire way.

Once parked, Cale came around and opened the door for her. She found the act endearing until she realized it was because he was really in a hurry. It wasn't his gentleman gene calling; it was his libido.

As soon as she slid out of the car, he had her by the elbow and was ushering her, rushing her, into the hotel. She didn't protest. The intense look on his face told her that it would do no good. He'd probably just growl at her.

They marched across the lobby to the elevators. Cale punched the up button several times. Olena had to stifle a laugh. He was clearly on the edge. She didn't want to push him off it quite yet. Maybe when they got into the elevator.

One of the six elevators opened, and Cale ushered her in. He banged on the close button before anyone else could get on. One unhappy lady let them know exactly how she was feeling as the doors shut in her face.

Olena let out a giggle then. "Did you see her face?" But her grin soon faded when Cale crowded into her, forcing her to back up into the wall. "What are you doing?"

"Taking what's mine."

"Excuse me?"

But he wasn't having any of her excuses or angry remarks. Cradling her face in the palms of his wide rough hands, Cale tilted her chin up and took her mouth.

A moan escaped her lips as he swept his tongue over hers, sampling her. Her knees nearly gave out at the power of the kiss. She reached out and fisted her hands in the front of his shirt so she wouldn't collapse. Little quivers rushed through her body. She felt weak and invigorated all at the same time. He possessed a power over her that she knew he didn't realize he had. She hoped he wouldn't figure it out or she'd be a goner.

As the elevator ascended, Cale continued to take her mouth, nipping and tugging at her lips and tongue. Her belly clenched tight and her thighs tingled in anticipation.

When they reached his floor, Cale took her by the hand again and led her down the hall to his room. She had to quicken her step to keep up with him. A fierce look crossed his face. It was the look of a man possessed. And it made her heart skip a few beats.

With his key card he opened the door and Olena went in. He followed her in and shut the door behind him. Just as she managed to turn around to face him, Cale wrapped his arms around her and kissed her again.

His hands were everywhere at once. Rubbing her back, caressing her rear end, undoing the buttons on her shirt. She could hardly catch her breath.

"I want to see your panties again," he murmured, as his fingers made quick work of her shirt. He parted the fabric and yanked it down her arms, his lips never leaving her face.

Next his hands were at the button of her pants. He undid it, and pulling away from her mouth, he knelt down and slowly pulled her pants down her legs. A hard and hot rush of pleasure surged through her as she glanced down at the top of his head. She could feel his hot breath on the flesh of her belly. He was breathing hard, as was she.

When her pants were at her ankles, he held them still while she stepped out of them. The act sent shivers up her spine. Starting at her calves, Cale moved his hands up her legs with just the lightest of touches. Her heart picked up several beats as his fingers stroked the outsides of her thighs.

"You're so damn beautiful, Olena. It makes me ache."

She couldn't respond. Words wouldn't form. Her throat was too dry for anything but a low moan.

Cale buried his face into her stomach, laving his tongue over her skin. Reaching down, she wove her fingers into his hair as he licked and caressed her body.

Her breath came out in ragged pants as his tongue dipped into her navel and ventured even lower. He ran his tongue along the edge of her lacy panties, making her flesh warm and tingly.

He slid a finger through the band around her leg and into her slick heat. She knew she was hot and wet for him, open to his touch. She watched him through the dark hood of her lashes as he stroked her up and down. Her legs shook from the effort to stay on her feet.

Taking hold of the waistband of her panties, he pulled them over her hips and down her legs. When she stepped out of them, he gripped her thigh in his hands and flipped her leg over his shoulder. She wrapped her hands tighter in his hair to hold on. He didn't give her a chance to take another breath before he laved his tongue between her legs.

Fierce, burning heat spread out over her flesh. Her entire body quaked from the inside out as Cale feasted on her. She'd felt desire before, many times, but this insatiable hunger was something new. It was as if his touch seared her to the core, ignited every inch of her body until she was a quivering mass of pure pleasure.

She ached for him to touch her everywhere, explore every crevice, every inch of her. She'd never felt this type of passion before. One that conquered her completely and made her want to drop to her knees and thank the god for sending Cale to her.

Again he stroked between her legs, adding his fingers into the mix. His thumb caressed her most sensitive spot. She could hardly breathe as the muscles in her thighs tightened. An explosive orgasm was building like a spinning tornado. It wouldn't take much more for her to come in a flood of ecstasy.

Gripping his hair for support, Olena looked down at Cale as he licked and suckled on her sex. Gone was the human agent who followed the rules. In his place was a wild, unfettered being intent on taking everything she could give him. She'd unleashed something she was unsure if she could handle. By the pleasure rushing over her body, she wouldn't mind the effort of trying.

As if sensing her need, Cale slipped two fingers deep inside her. He swirled them around, burying them deep, feeling all of her.

Sweat trickled down between her breasts. Her thighs tightened in anticipation. Her gut churned, knowing it would be soon. Gripping his hair tighter, Olena worried her bottom lip with her fangs. The beginning flutters of orgasm rushed through her.

Sensing that she was close, Cale increased the pressure, teasing her sensitive nerves. One more suck, one more lick, one more push with his fingers was all it took for her to come crashing down.

Moaning, Olena rode his mouth, pumping her hips with every wave of pleasure. It had been too long since she'd experienced a climax so intense, so vehement. Shc could do nothing but hang on to Cale as surge after surge of ecstasy crashed over hcr.

When her tremors had subsided, Cale got to his feet. His gaze was dark and fierce and his lips were swollen and slick with her desire. After all that, he didn't look any tamer than he'd been when they first got in the car and drove to his hotel. In fact, he looked more determined than ever. The thought actually scared her a little.

He scared her. On all kinds of levels.

He threatened her independent way of life. The life she'd built for herself after her last husband had died. She swore then she'd never fall in love again. Never give her heart and her soul to a man. Not ever. But with Cale it was getting harder and harder to keep that promise to herself. He was chipping away at her walls, at her defenses. Her heart was in jeopardy. And that was the most frightening thing of all.

"I'm not done with you," he growled as he grabbed her by the arm and pulled her another two feet into the living room.

Whipping her around so her back nestled into his front, he pushed her up against the sofa. The fronts of her thighs banged up against the back of the sofa. And before she could say anything, he bent her over the cushions.

Chapter 21

"What are you doing?" she chirped. He could hear the panic in her voice. He smiled, knowing he'd driven her to this, pushed her past her limits.

"Having you."

Her gaze lit up like green fire as he stroked his hands over the cheeks of her heart-shaped ass. He'd heard that vampires' eyes glowed when they were afflicted with intense emotions, but he'd never seen it before now. His stomach clenched at the sight. He'd done this to her.

Cale loved her like this. All vulnerable and under his control. But he wasn't under any delusion that he'd taken it from her. Shc had absolutely handed it over to him. He loved that she trusted him like this.

And he was going to take full advantage of it.

Keeping her pinned to the sofa, Cale unbuttoned his pants and shucked them down his legs. He was blistering hot and hard for her. Situating himself right at her juncture, he spread her and slid himself in.

She was hot and wet and open for him. It took everything he had not to ram himself deep. He bit his lip with restraint as he thrust into her. She moaned deep in her throat while he established his rhythm.

In and out. At first slow and easy, torturing her as well as himself. Then he couldn't restrain himself any longer and he was pumping hard. Digging his fingers into her hips, he buried himself deep, then withdrew, only to do it again and again, until sweat dripped off his forehead and soaked the front and back of his dress shirt.

It wasn't long before his stomach and thigh muscles clenched in preparation. Pitching forward, he covered Olena's back and thrust deep inside her. He clamped his eyes shut, but it didn't stop the explosion of white behind his lids when he came.

His release was fierce and hot and intense, and he wasn't sure how to handle it. He could hear her heart thumping hard and hear the labor in her breathing. He opened his eyes and looked down at her. Her head was to the side and he could see that she wasn't smiling, but she wasn't frowning, either. Her look was one of utter fury.

He straightened, and slipping out of her, he quickly reached down and pulled on his pants. She'd yet to move, was still sprawled over the back of the sofa, her legs still spread. He noticed red marks at her hips where his fingers had dug in. The cheeks of her rear end were a slight pink from his brutal pounding.

"I'm sorry," he said as he wiped the sweat from his brow.

Straightening, she turned and glared at him. "Don't you dare say sorry for this. You can apologize for being an ass, but don't you dare be sorry for screwing me."

He stared at her, unsure of what to say in return. She looked angry, but from what she'd just said she wasn't mad about having sex with him. Why did this have to be so complicated? He'd damn well known this was going to happen between them. Complications. Miscommunications. Problems. Ones he didn't want.

"Okay."

"If I didn't want to have sex with you, Cale, I wouldn't have let you." She marched over to where her panties and her pants had been discarded and picked them up. "Don't look so distraught. You didn't hurt me. You didn't sully my impeccable reputation. Get over yourself. You're not that wicked."

Taking her clothes, she marched into the bathroom and slammed the door shut.

He walked to the door, intending to pull it open and give her a piece of his mind, but didn't. Instead he pressed his hand against the wood jamb and sighed. He'd behaved foolishly. In a jealous fit. He didn't realize how out of control she made him until now. He was acting and reacting before thinking. That wasn't something he normally did, but being around Olena pushed him to his limits. Obviously, pushed him beyond them.

He swung away from the bathroom door and went back into the living room. He collapsed onto the sofa and ran his hands over his face and head. He had to pull himself together if he was going to be of any further use on this case. Interpol was counting on him; his boss was counting on him. And if he was right in his assumption about terrorist activities, maybe this whole city was counting on him.

Sex with Olena had been incredible. Instead of sating him, though, it just made him want more. Hell, he still wanted her, even now.

Sitting back on the sofa, he closed his eyes and sighed. The scent of her skin and of her desire floated to his nose. He inhaled it deep and knew that putting Olena out of his mind was going to be damn near impossible.

Twenty minutes later, Cale was once again sitting on the sofa. Olena was in the armchair, waiting for him to glean something from the silver bracelet Ivy had dropped at the safe house.

He held it tight in his right fist. Closing his eyes, he took a deep breath and started to rub his thumb over the metal. It warmed to his touch. Soon it became so warm that he knew there'd be a red patch on his skin when he was through.

Images flashed through his mind at record speed. He could barely discern anything concrete.

An apple.

Olena's face.

Darkness, then white, like a strobe light.

Tick's pale face.

An old woman missing two front teeth.

A broken-down room with wooden boards across the destroyed windows. Between two slats are the words Midnight Blue.

A dark street. Flickering streetlights.

Bright-colored lights. People in various levels of undress dancing. Moving up against each other.

A small room. A desk.

And Valentino. Angry. Yelling. Threatening.

Lifting his hand as if to strike.

Ice. A cube of cool ice.

Cale opened his eyes and let the bracelet drop from his fingers and onto the coffee table. He looked down into his palm. He'd been right about the heat. His skin was scorched bright pink. He flexed his fingers, the pain now just starting to shoot up his arm.

"What did you see?"

"Valentino. He's been threatening her. I think he's involved with whatever is going on."

"Anything about what was in the safety-deposit box?"

He shook his head, unclear on exactly what

he'd seen and what he could understand. "I don't know. There was something about ice."

"Ice? As in frozen water?"

"I don't know. The word *ice* was in Ivy's mind while Valentino was yelling at her. I had a sense it was something important to her."

"Maybe it's a code word for something."

"Could be."

"Anything else?"

He frowned, trying to piece the images together. "A run-down building. A room with boarded-up windows. And through the slats something about midnight blue."

Olena worried her bottom lip as she was thinking. After a few moments her eyes lit up. "There's an old movie theater downtown called the Midnight Blue. There arc several run-down buildings near there."

"Maybe she's living in one."

Olena nodded. "It's worth a look."

Nodding, Cale stood, still flexing his fingers. "But first I need to wrap my hand." He went into the bathroom, where he kept his first aid kit.

He was unzipping the bag when Olena came in. She took it from him and found the roll of gauze. Then she took his hand in hers and slowly wrapped him up. When she was done, she brought his hand up to her mouth and kissed it.

"Better?"

"Much." He smiled and nodded. "Olena, I—"

She set her fingers over his lips to stop his words. "Don't ruin a perfectly good bonding moment."

He laughed. "Okay, I won't."

"Good. I'm getting exhausted trying to keep this relationship on an even keel. Quit trying to complicate things."

He nodded in agreement. But he got the feeling that she didn't quite believe her own words. Things between them were complicated. And Olena was fooling herself if she thought differently.

She could play the cool customer, the one indifferent to their growing relationship, but he felt the power of her emotions when she looked at him. Some things a person couldn't hide. But if she chose to hide them from herself, he wouldn't stop her. At least not right now.

When the case was over, they'd have some major things to work out between them.

"Did you call Gabriel?" he asked, getting back to work. "Were they able to pick Valentino up?"

She shook her head. "He wasn't home."

"We need to get a warrant for his club. I bet that's where he's hiding out."

"Most likely."

They went back into the living room. Cale slid on his holster and suit jacket. "We can call Gabriel on the way back downtown. See if we can get a crew together to find him."

Fifteen minutes later, they had parked the car near the old Midnight Blue theater and were walking across the street toward the dilapidated building on the corner. When Cale looked up, he saw that several windows facing the theater were boarded up. This definitely seemed like the place from his vision.

The front door wasn't broken or locked. It was still surprisingly intact. Olena peered through the dirty window. "Looks okay."

She pulled open the door and walked in. Cale followed behind. Inside was a lobby, or what used to be one, for the apartments above. Now it was dirty, smelly and a big old playroom for bugs. Several cockroaches were racing across the cracked linoleum.

In the far corner, in the deep shadows, was an easy chair that at one time had been a luxury item.

Now it was faded, frayed and patched up with duct tape. But it was who was sitting in the chair that drew Cale's attention.

Cale grabbed Olena's arm and motioned toward the corner.

Ivy stood up, her hair in complete disarray. She looked worse than she had when they'd seen her last. With her head downcast, she shuffled toward them. They met her halfway.

"I'm sorry I bailed on you."

Up close, Cale could see the dark circles around her eyes. Her face looked even more gaunt, if that was possible. She looked like a skeleton of who she was.

"Do you want to talk to us now?" Olena asked.

The girl nodded. "I'm ready to tell you everything."

Chapter 22

They managed to settle Ivy into an interview room. Not one of those sterile rooms where they usually put suspects or people of interest. Ivy was neither, but she was definitely a key person in this case.

Gabriel had gotten her a sandwich, some coffee and a chocolate bar from one of the vending machines. He set them on the table for her and then retreated to the corner of the room. She barely glanced at him as she tore at the sandwich package.

Olena and Cale sat in chairs on the opposite

side of the table. A court-appointed child advocate, who had to be brought in because of Ivy's age, sat beside her.

The advocate had warned them to go slow with the questions, but Olena felt they were long past that. They had to get some real answers for this case. Dancing around the subject wasn't going to find Luc Dubois's killer, or the people who blew up the bank. It wasn't going to help Ivy, either. The sooner they could figure this out, the sooner she could inherit her uncle's wealth and move on to a healthier life.

"Do you know who killed your uncle?"

The advocate sneered. "Ms. Petrovich, I warned you about this."

Ivy ignored her remarks. "No. But I know why he was killed."

"Why?" Cale prompted.

"Because of something I did." She unwrapped the candy bar and started to nibble on the end.

"What was that, Ivy?"

"I made something for Uncle Luc. Something that the others wanted badly. They were going to pay him a lot of money for it."

Olena glanced at Cale. She wondered if his

theory was right. That Ivy harnessed her magical energy into a makeshift bomb.

"What did you make?"

The advocate put her hand on top of Ivy's. "You don't have to answer, Ivy. You can ask for a lawyer."

"No, it's okay. I realize now I have to tell the truth. I have to for my uncle."

Olena nodded to her to go ahead.

"I'm really good with computers. Uncle Luc said I had computer magic. I can operate and hack into any system, anywhere, anytime. It isn't hard for me at all. I can see all the codes in my head and my fingers just type them in."

Olena thought that now Otto's comment about overhearing Luc talk on the phone about computers made sense.

"He asked me to create a virus for him. A really nasty virus that could wipe out all the systems in the world."

"And did you?" Cale asked. Olena could tell he was excited. This was what he'd been looking for all along.

She nodded then licked her lips. "I did it. It didn't take me long. Like a day or so. I called it ICE, because it can freeze any computer system anywhere and give control back to the creator."

Olena shared another look with Cale. She hadn't expected this revelation from the girl. A computer virus. All of this was over a way to control the Internet. But she supposed it made sense in today's society, where everything was digital—from retail to banking to the country's defense systems. She shuddered. One touch and some terrorist organization could have control over the world.

"But Uncle Luc never gave them the disc."

Olena turned back to Ivy. "What?"

"I gave it to him, but he decided not to go through with the sale. After I found out what he was planning on doing with it I begged him not to. He finally listened to me." She gave them a small sad smile.

"To whom did he plan to give the disc?" Cale asked her.

She shook her head. "I don't know."

"Where is the disc now?" he continued.

"In a safe place."

Cale leaned forward on the table, but Olena grabbed his arm and squeezed lightly before he could demand that Ivy give them the disc. He glanced at her and she shook her head. He sat back but crossed his arms over his chest.

Olena asked the next question. "Did Valentino know about the disc?"

She nodded.

"Did he tell you to give it to him after Luc was killed?"

"He said he'd tell the cops what I'd done if I didn't give it to him. He said I'd go to jail for the rest of my life." She looked so small as she spoke, Olena wanted to reach across the table and hold her hand. "Am I going to jail?"

"No. You're not going to go to jail, Ivy. I won't let that happen." And she meant it. She'd do whatever she had to so this girl didn't spend one night in any kind of institution.

"Did Valentino threaten to harm you?" Cale asked.

She shook her head. "No. Not in any real sense. He couldn't, anyway. I'm a better witch than he is. That pisses him off quite a bit." She smiled.

Olena smiled in return. The girl had spirit, that was for sure.

"Do you think he killed your uncle?" Cale asked.

"I don't know. I don't want to think that he did. I thought they were best friends." Tears started to well in her eyes.

Olena couldn't stand it anymore. This time she

did reach across the table and grab Ivy's hand. The girl smiled up at her. "Thank you for being brave, Ivy."

"Did I help? Will you find whoever killed Uncle Luc?"

"You helped us immensely."

She nodded, and the tears fell.

Ten minutes later, Olena and Cale met with Gabriel in his office. The advocate had taken Ivy to another of their safe houses. Now that Olena had been cleansed of the tracking spell Valentino had put on her, there was no way he or anyone else was going to find the girl. They'd asked Ivy several more times to tell them where the disc was, but she'd refused. She'd told them she didn't think anyone should have it. Olena understood the girl's motives, but when the time came she'd insist that Ivy give them the virus.

"I'd say we have enough to get a warrant for Valentino," Olena said.

"We have to be careful. Valentino has a few political friends," Gabriel said.

Olena swore. "I hate politics. I hated it during the French Revolution and I despise it now."

Cale coughed into his hand, but Olena could tell he was stifling a laugh.

Gabriel didn't hide his grin. "I know, but we want to get this guy and not have him get off on a technicality. If he's involved with the bank heist and the Dubois murder, we'll get him."

"I'm sure there's a judge who hates politics, too. You must know someone."

"Judge Randall Terry likes to shake it up once in a while."

"Then call him."

Gabriel picked up his phone. "Give me a minute." He swiveled around in his chair to make the call.

Cale leaned over to Olena. "What do you think?"

"I think that poor girl has been through a lot."

"Yeah, poor kid. But damn, to have that kind of power at your fingertips." He shook his head. "I couldn't even imagine it."

"It's not her fault that she's gifted."

"I didn't say it was. But I'm sure that once this gets out there will be others interested in what she can do."

She swiveled in her chair. "What are you saying? That Interpol will want to use her?"

He shrugged. "I don't know for sure, but she'd be extremely useful in our computer crimes division."

"Is that all we Otherworlders are to you humans? Useful?" She knew she was being unfair to him, but she couldn't help the surge of anger she felt. Ivy had been through hell.

Cale flinched away from her. "Whoa. Where did that come from? Is this about you and me?"

"No, this isn't about you and me. Why would it be?"

"I don't know. I just thought, you know, from earlier..."

"Why, is that how you feel about me? That I'm just useful? I'm only good for—" She eyed Gabriel. His back was still to them, but she knew he'd heard every word they were saying, even the unspoken ones. "Forget it," she finished. Sighing, she ran a hand through her hair and rubbed her head. A headache was starting to build. "I'm tired and I'm hungry."

Gabriel swiveled back around and hung up the phone. "We'll get our warrant, but it'll be a couple of hours." He looked from Olena to Cale and back to Olena. "You both look like you need a break. From each other, maybe?"

Cale stood. "I need to make a few phone calls." As he passed behind her chair, she could feel his eyes on her. She could sense that he wanted to say something to her, but Gabriel's presence stopped him. She didn't relax until she knew he'd left the room.

She sagged back into the chair and looked at Gabriel.

He was shaking his head at her.

"What?" she demanded.

"You know what. I thought you had more discretion than that, Olena."

She waved her hand at him. "Oh, bull. You know I don't have any."

He smiled at that, and she returned the gesture.

"Are you…in trouble?" he asked gently. She knew what he meant. What the real question was. Are you in love with this man?

"I might be, Gabriel."

"What are you going to do about it?"

She shook her head, feeling lost and alone. "I don't know. Forget about it right now, I guess. Until this case is solved."

"Then what?"

"Then we'll see, won't we?"

He didn't say anything, just gave her one of his sympathetic looks.

She stood. "I'm going to go finish up some paperwork. Come find me when we get the warrant."

"Sure thing."

Olena left Gabriel's office and walked down the hall to her own little piece of solitude. She had a desk in a small room that she shared with Sophie and Kellen. Thankfully, both of them were absent. She really needed some time alone to think and to decompress.

She sat in her chair and rubbed her head again. The pain was getting worse, her temples now throbbed. She pushed past it and tried to focus on the case, which, thankfully, was finally rolling ahead.

So was her and Cale's relationship. Something had changed between them, and she wasn't sure she liked it much.

She was a woman used to having control and wielding power, but she didn't feel either of these things right now. In fact, she felt vulnerable and weak. Two emotions she hadn't experienced in a long time.

She liked Cale, but she wasn't sure she was willing to open herself that wide for him. She knew he wasn't the type of man who would settle for half or even three-quarters of her heart. He'd demand the whole thing.

Sighing, she closed her eyes and rubbed her

temples. She was hungry. She needed some nutrients. With any luck, the vending machine would be stocked with her favorite type.

"I thought you might need this."

Olena swiveled in her chair to see Cale leaning in the doorway, a bottle of blood dangling from his fingers.

"I thought you had phone calls to make."

"I made them." He came into the room and set the bottle onto her desk. It was AB positive, her favorite.

She picked up the bottle, unscrewed the cap and took a big swallow. She smiled. "How did you know what I preferred?"

"I'm observant."

After saluting him with the bottle, she finished the rest. "Thank you."

"You're welcome. You looked like you needed it."

"I didn't realize I was so easy to read."

"Oh, you're not. Trust me." He came around behind her chair and set his hands on her shoulders. She was about to protest when he started to massage her aching muscles. She hadn't realized how truly tense she was until Cale worked those twisted knots.

"Oh, that feels good," she moaned, letting her head fall forward.

He stroked her neck up and down, kneading the tension out with strong manipulations. She didn't think she'd ever had as good a massage as the one he was giving her. It might've been purely because she needed it or because it was Cale doing the massaging. She accepted that it was probably a little of both.

"I didn't tell Interpol about Ivy."

She lifted her head but didn't respond.

"Although I think her gifts would be useful, I'm not going to be the one who uses her. I just wanted you to know that."

She lifted her hands and rested them over his. "I'm sorry if I accused you of anything. I know you'd never do that."

He spun her around in her chair and cradled her head in his hands. "You're important to me, Olena. I don't want our jobs to put us at odds with each other."

"I don't, either." She wasn't sure what else to say. There were words in her head, but she wasn't sure if now was the right time to let them out.

He tilted her head up and bent down to press his lips to hers.

"Uh, am I interrupting?"

Breaking apart, they both looked toward the door where Gabriel stood in the threshold, one eyebrow raised in question.

Cale straightened and let his hands fall to his sides. Olena stood, trying hard not to show that she was very close to succumbing to Cale's attentions.

Gabriel raised his hand. In it, he had a piece of paper. "We have our warrant."

Chapter 23

They decided it would be best to hit the club before it opened. That way they wouldn't have any problems with crowd control, especially if Valentino decided to run. Which Cale figured would be most likely.

He, Olena, Gabriel and three constables took their positions outside the club preparing to execute the warrant. Carrying it out took more than just getting a piece of paper. They needed to prepare for any eventual magic issues, as well as lycan problems, so François had given them all protection amulets to wear. Olena didn't think

Otto would stand in their way. On the contrary, he would probably be very interested to know that Valentino had something to do with his lover's demise.

Gabriel knocked twice on the red door.

At first, he thought no one was going to answer, then came a series of clanks and clicks, an indication of locks being opened, and a big burly lycan bouncer pulled the door open.

"The place is closed. Come back later."

Gabriel showed him the paper. "We have a warrant to search the place."

"For what?"

"For Valentino DeCosta."

"He's not here."

"We'd still like to look around." Gabriel nodded to the constable, who then stepped up and grabbed the lycan's arm.

"Can you step outside please, sir?"

At first, Cale thought the lycan was going to put up a struggle, but he surveyed all of them and likely decided he wasn't going to win. Gabriel could no doubt kick the big guy's butt. The inspector had that feral way about him.

Once the lycan was removed from the doorway, Gabriel moved into the club, followed by Olena and Cale. Cale didn't want to be too far from her. He knew things could go wrong real fast and he wanted to protect her. Although in this situation, with all kinds of Otherworld beings around him, it was likely he who needed protection. He was just too much of a man, human in all ways, to accept that fact.

The place was empty except for a few people milling about around the bar and the DJ booth. With the lights on and the music off, Cale didn't think the place looked all that enchanting.

As they crossed the floor, there were plenty of curious gazes, but no one made a move to stop them.

Before they could reach the red door, though, it opened and Otto came out, obviously warned by one of his employees. Or possibly he sensed that they'd arrived. Vampires had all kinds of powers that Cale was just beginning to fully understand.

"What's going on?" He asked the question of Olena, as she was the only vampire among them.

"We're here for Valentino."

Otto's face darkened. "Are you saying he had something to do with Luc's death?"

"It's likely."

"I don't believe it."

"He's been tracking Ivy, and we have some evidence that suggests he's been after whatever was in Luc's safety-deposit box and it is the reason that Luc was murdered."

He shook his head in disbelief, but Cale figured the vampire had to have suspected at least some of it. He seemed like a smart man. Valentino couldn't be operating under this guy's radar without at least some suspicion.

"Is Valentino here?" Gabriel asked. He lifted the paper. "We have a warrant for his arrest."

The vampire shook his head. "I haven't seen him since you were here before."

Cale thought he was lying. Otto's eyes shifted to the side, avoiding Olena's intense gaze.

"We will get justice for Luc, Otto," Olena said, obviously sensing what Cale had. "Let us do our job. Please don't take it into your own hands."

He turned back to her. "I said he wasn't here."

"We're going to look around, anyway," Gabriel said. "Could you please step out of the way?"

He did so, albeit reluctantly. He glared at each of them as they passed him and stepped through the door leading to the back offices.

The moment they were all through, Gabriel,

Olena, Cale and the two constables, the door slammed shut behind them and the lights went out. They were plunged into total darkness.

Cale reached out for Olena. His hands filled with air and nothing else. "Olena!"

There was no response. How could that be? Where had she gone? Surely someone would've responded to him—Gabriel or one of the constables.

Groping blindly, Cale felt for the wall, another person, anything to gain his bearings. He put one foot in front of the other, counting off steps. By the tenth one he realized he should've hit something. The corridor hadn't been that wide or long.

This had to have been some sort of spell. Valentino had set something up in the event that they showed up. And Otto had allowed them to walk right into it. Maybe he was even in on it from the beginning and killed his longtime lover out of greed. Regardless of species, males were driven to action by money, power or sex. Take your pick.

And like a guileless fool, Cale had forgotten to put his amulet around his neck. It was in his coat pocket, not realizing it needed to touch his skin to work. Desperate and confused, Cale kept moving through the absolute dark. The only thing that was solid was the floor beneath his feet. But he was afraid that if he crouched to feel it with his fingers it, too, would disappear into oblivion. If that happened, would he fall into a void?

He wondered if the others were experiencing the same thing he was. Was Olena lost in her own dark world? He imagined she was faring better, though. She at least could see in the dark with her vampire eyes.

He'd experienced a lot in his life and in his career with Interpol, but nothing had prepared him for this. No amount of torture training or investigation into the minds of Otherworlders could have prepared him to be trapped in darkness with no frame of reference to draw on, nothing to lean against and draw strength from. He was wandering around deaf, dumb and blind.

"You're not afraid of the dark, are you, Agent Braxton?"

The voice came from everywhere and nowhere all at once. Cale spun around in circles trying to pinpoint its location.

"Round and round you go, where you stop, nobody knows." The voice cackled. It was then he realized it belonged to one Valentino DeCosta.

"I'll find you, you son of a bitch."

There came another cackle. "No, you won't. You can't even find yourself."

The last two words were whispered as if Valentino had spoken them right into his ear. Cale spun around, his heart racing. Panic was starting to settle in. What if he couldn't ever get out of this black hole? What if he was stuck here forever, damned to walk aimlessly in the dark?

Olena was out there, either wondering where he'd gone or in her own hell. He couldn't fathom not seeing her again. It had never crossed his mind that he wouldn't get another chance to hold her, to kiss her, to make love to her. He'd thought he had all the time in the world to tell her how he felt about her. That maybe, just maybe, he was going against everything he thought possible and was falling in love with her.

But now he might've missed his opportunity.

Swinging around, anger swirling in his gut, Cale waved his hands back and forth trying desperately to touch something. Something to cushion the blow that came to his heart and to his soul with the notion that Olena was lost to him forever.

"Come out and fight me, you coward."

Again, came the manic chuckle. "What's the

matter, Braxton, feeling lonely? Don't worry. I've taken care of the lovely Olena. She won't miss you, I promise you that."

"I'm going to kill you, DeCosta."

"Please, what can you do to me, human? Absolutely nothing. You are powerless here."

"Say that to my face."

The chuckle again, but this time it wasn't so hearty. Maybe he was wearing the witch down.

"Olena was just playing with you, Agent. You know you couldn't possibly fulfill a woman who has lived so long and so well. In a few weeks' time, she'll have moved on and you'll be just a small piece of her long repertoire."

Cale tried not to listen, tried not to let the words sink in. But he'd pondered the same things.

"You're a coward, Valentino. You can't even track down one little girl. And it just pissed you off that she's a far better witch than you'll ever be."

"You know, I tire of your banter." There was a heavy sigh. Cale could feel the puff of air on the back of his neck. Maybe he wasn't as alone as he thought he was.

He swung around, his fist raised. But it was too late.

"Sleep."

With that one word, Cale collapsed into unconsciousness.

Chapter 24

"Where the hell is he?" Olena ran up and down the corridor searching in every room, every corner, every nook, looking for Cale.

"Calm down, Olena. We'll find him." Gabriel tried to grab her arm as she whizzed past him to search the office again.

"You don't know that," she said.

"He's not dead. If he was, we would've found a body. So if he's not dead, we can find him."

She was in a panic. She could feel it bubbling inside her. She'd been in this state ever since the lights had gone out briefly, then flashed back on, revealing that Cale was gone. He'd just vanished.

"Valentino set this trap."

"Yes, that much is obvious." Gabriel grabbed the knob on the door and tried to turn it. It was locked. "It seems we're locked in."

With an angry sigh, Olena stomped over to the door, wrapped her hand around the doorknob and cranked it. Instantly the handle came off in her hand along with the locking mechanism. She tossed it to the side and kicked open the door. The frame cracked from the force of the blow.

They marched out into the club. Two bartenders were milling about the bar, setting up shop. Olena stomped over to them, fury making her eyes glow.

"Where's Otto?"

They both looked at her wearily. Then one nodded toward the DJ booth. Smart man. She swirled around and marched toward the booth. Otto saw her coming through the bulletproof window.

He met her at the door. "Is there a prob—"

That was all he could get out before Olena had him pressed against the wall by his throat with his feet dangling in midair.

"Where is he?"

He clawed at her hand, but it was to no avail. "I don't know."

"Where did he take Cale?"

He frowned then. "Who?"

"Agent Braxton. Where did Valentino take him?"

He shook his head, still clawing at her arm. Fueled by righteous anger, she had no intention of letting go. She didn't even feel his nails furrowing her flesh. She could see the blood dripping down her arm, but she didn't care one bit. It was nothing compared to the pain ripping her apart inside.

Gabriel grabbed her by the shoulder. "Let him go, Olena. You're not helping matters."

She released her hold on Otto's throat and let him drop to the floor. He didn't fall, though. He was much too agile for that.

Rubbing his throat, he said, "I'm sure you're going to explain to me why I'm not going to press charges against you for assault."

"A spell was triggered when we went through the door, and Agent Braxton was kidnapped," Olena growled, her hands still shaking. "You can't tell me you didn't know about it."

"I assure you I did not."

"I don't believe you."

"Well, that is a shame."

Gabriel stepped up. "We are taking you in for questioning, Otto."

One constable came along the vampire's side and gestured for him to go ahead.

Otto nodded once to him, then to Olena. "I hope you find your agent. I can see that he means a lot to you."

Olena didn't watch as he was escorted out of the building. She didn't want to believe that he hadn't had anything to do with Cale's disappearance. She wanted someone to pay. If it couldn't be Valentino right now, she'd take anyone.

Gabriel patted her shoulder. "Let's go look at the scene. Maybe we can find something that will help us."

Together they walked back to the broken door and corridor to the back offices. She peered down the hallway. "How did he do it?"

Gabriel joined her. "A trap of some sort."

"A spell." She stepped over the fallen door and back into the hallway. She examined the floor. "It had to be triggered somehow. It had to be tuned into Cale."

"Maybe it was random."

She shook her head. "I think it was deliberate."

"But why Cale?"

"Because he has more at stake then we do and fewer defenses." She spied something on the floor. Crouching, she picked it up between her fingers. It was a gold cuff link. One of Cale's cuff links. She'd seen it on him a couple of days ago. She showed it to Gabriel.

"Now the question is, did he drop it when he vanished or was it used for a spell?"

"He wasn't wearing cuff links today."

"How did Valentino get it off Cale to use it?"

She took out a plastic evidence bag from her jacket pocket, then dropped the link in, sealing it shut tightly. She deposited it back into her pocket and started to pace the corridor.

"When we were here last time, Valentino shook our hands right before we left. He could've taken it then. He's an expert at sleight of hand. Just like he planted that tracking spell on me, he could've easily taken Cale's cuff link."

"But what does it gain him?"

"Leverage." Olena said. She hated to say it, but she knew it to be true. Cale had been taken because he was human. Because he would've been the easiest to take. And he'd be the easiest to get information out of.

Gabriel looked at her. And she knew he understood what she was thinking. He nodded to her. "He's tough. He's had extensive training in all types of interrogation techniques, both human and Otherworlder."

"I know, but magic, Gabriel. That is one thing he couldn't possibly be immune to. Valentino will use everything at his disposal, including black magic. I've seen what that kind of torture can do to a person. Most don't come back from it."

He rested his hand on her shoulder again. "He will. You'll see. He's one tough SOB. I know people, Olena. And Cale Braxton will come back in one piece. He will for you."

She nodded, pressing her lips together. Though she really wanted to cry, she instead squared her shoulders up and swiveled around to the crime scene to get to work. She couldn't help Cale by standing around feeling sorry for herself. She had to dig deep and find something that could help him. Find the clue that would lead her to him.

Because once she found it, hell itself wouldn't

be able to stop her from getting to him. She would knock down everything and everyone in her way. Especially Valentino DeCosta.

Chapter 25

Cale blinked open his eyes to darkness. But it wasn't the complete, oppressive black like before. This time when his eyes adjusted he could make out a few things around him.

He was in a small room lying on the floor. Cool, hard cement by the feel of it on his back.

Stripped of his watch, also his jacket and tie, he didn't know how long he'd been lying on the floor unconscious. He didn't think it had been that long, as his muscles hadn't quite stiffened up yet.

He tried to sit up but his head pounded at the

intrusive movement. It felt like he'd been knocked in the back of the head, but when his fingers inspected his skull he found no blood or bump. Then he remembered Valentino's eerily detached voice. When he'd spoken the word *sleep,* Cale had dropped. Maybe it was magic making his head throb as if he'd been out on a bender with his mates for a week straight.

He got to his feet, albeit shakily, and searched for a door. The darkness was thick, so he had to use his hands to feel along the walls. Eventually, along the far wall he found the outline of a door and a doorknob. But when he touched the handle with his right hand he experienced a jolt to his system like electricity. It shot him back a few feet.

Shaky, he felt along the door again. His hand was numb and he could barely feel his fingers as they pressed against the wood. He dug his fingers into the groove of the door but there was no way he could pry it open without a tool. It was useless. There was no way out. He was stuck in the room until someone came to get him.

Cale settled himself again on the floor leaning against the wall, his knees up. He'd sit and prepare himself for whatever came next. It was obvious now that he'd been taken for a reason.

Ransom most likely. A trade-off for Ivy and the virus. It was standard procedure not to negotiate with terrorists, so Cale knew he was on his own.

He wondered how Olena was doing. Was she scouring the city for him? His ego made him consider it, but in reality he knew she'd do the right thing, the logical thing, and try and follow the evidence. If there was any. He liked to think she'd want to trade the girl and virus for him, but he knew she wouldn't. She was a professional.

She would do everything she could to find him, he knew, but in the end she would do what was right.

Rubbing his hands over his face, he tried to erase the remnants of the grogginess he felt. He'd need his strength and his wits if he was going to survive. Once they realized that the NMPD wasn't going to trade him, he'd become expendable. And they'd get rid of him, quickly and quietly, covering their tracks as they did so.

Cale wasn't going to make it easy for them. He was trained in several fighting styles and could kill a man with a few well-placed moves. Killing a lycan or a vampire was another matter altogether, but he knew a few things that could take down any man, no matter what species. All men were vulnerable in certain spots on their bodies, whether they had fangs or grew furry during a full moon. He might not kill them, but at least he could stun them and maybe give himself some time to escape.

While he was pondering this, the door creaked open and the doorway filled with two very large bodies.

"Wakey, wakey, eggs and bakey," said one of the bruisers as he stepped into the room. The other one followed behind.

Cale was on his feet in seconds, preparing to fight.

"Valentino wants to talk," the first bruiser said. The other one smiled, revealing several tiny pointed teeth.

Lycans, the both of them. He was going to have one hell of a fight on his hands.

"Come on, human, and make it easier on yourself."

Cale took a step back with his right leg and settled his hands at his waist, looking for an opening. They were both really big, muscular but not fat. One he might be able to injure, but two were next to impossible. Despite all this, every fiber of his being told him to fight.

They circled him, obviously sensing he wasn't going to go quietly. In their arrogance they left an opening between them. It was a small opening, but one nonetheless. He had to take the chance.

"Come on, little human. Don't make me collar you and drag you out the door." The big bruiser took another step toward Cale.

It was just enough room for him to dash between them. Without another thought, Cale pushed off with his right leg and dove between the two lycans, rolling on the floor and coming up near the door. He sprinted over the threshold and kept running. He was maybe ten feet down a dark empty hall when one of the lycans was on him.

He took the fierce blow in the lower back. It took his legs out from underneath him. The pain exploded through his body and he crumpled to the ground. He'd be surprised if that hit hadn't busted something inside. Rolling over to get up, he could barely breathe.

But the lycan kicked him in the side before he could sit up. Then the other lycan arrived and they took turns kicking him from side to side like a soccer ball. After about the fifth kick, Cale stopped feeling them. His whole body was just one giant mass of dark agony.

Curling into a ball, his arms over his face, he swirled in and out of consciousness until finally, blissfully, the darkness took him under.

The sting of icy water jerked him awake. Sputtering to catch his breath, he noticed that he was in another room, a larger one, tied tightly to a wooden chair. He twitched a little to test his bonds. They were secure. He wasn't going anywhere.

Even that small move sent a rush of stabbing, agonizing pain through him. It nearly made him retch. His vision was impaired; everything seemed blurry, as if he was peering through a dirty window.

"Hello, Agent Braxton."

Cale lifted his head to see Valentino leaning against a long wooden table. Though the image wavered in and out of focus, Cale could tell exactly who it was. Valentino was dressed casually but still with a wealthy flair.

"You're a tricky little man, aren't you?"

Cale ignored the barb and surveyed his surroundings. There were a couple of high windows in the room. They were blacked out with what looked like spray paint. Then he must be in an area where Valentino feared nosy neighbors. Maybe there was hope yet to get out of this situation.

"I need to ask you a few questions."

Cale dropped his head to his chest. He couldn't hold it up any longer. He was having a difficult time even staying conscious.

More cold water was splashed over him. It cleared his head a little, but the iciness stole his breath.

"Don't fall asleep on me now, Agent Braxton. You have to answer some questions for me. Then you can go to sleep for as long as you want." There was that manic giggle again.

Cale raised his head and glared at Valentino. "And what if I don't feel like talking? Are you going to have your two goons beat me again?"

Valentino smiled, shaking his head. "No. That would be too easy for you. You've probably had hours and hours of conditioning for that exact situation." A giggle. "No, I have something even better for you." He nodded toward the open door. "Bring her in."

One of the big bruisers came into the room. With him, struggling against his hold, was a woman. A woman with long sable-colored hair and vivid green eyes.

"Olena!" Cale called.

She struggled even more. "Cale," she shouted.

The lycan wrapped his big meaty hand around her neck and pushed her to her knees.

"Oh, isn't this sweet," Valentino said. "You two make quite the couple."

Cale could barely contain himself. He pulled and twisted on the ropes binding him to the chair. It did nothing but chafe and burn his skin. Every movement sent jolts of pain zinging down his body. The pain was making his head swim, but he didn't care. He couldn't let Valentino hurt Olena. And he knew without a doubt that was exactly what he had planned.

The witch pushed away from the table and went to stand in front of Olena. "Now, I can see by your face, Cale, that you know exactly what I am capable of. So here is how this is going to work. I'm going to ask you a question. If you don't answer me, or if I think you are lying, I'm going to hurt your lady here."

"I'm going to kill you," Cale hissed.

Valentino shook his head. "Don't be stupid. That's not part of the game. Do you want me to explain the rules to you again?" He grabbed Olena by the hair and plowed his other hand into her face, right into her mouth.

The punching sound reverberated around the

room. Squeezing his eyes shut, Cale twisted in his chair, pulling his hands so hard he felt his shoulder pop out of joint. Sweat poured down his forehead and soaked his shirt. He opened his eyes and winced when he saw blood coating Olena's chin from her busted lip.

"Ask your damn questions."

"Do you have Ivy Seaborn in custody?"

He glanced at Olena. She was staring at him, her eyes almost begging him. For what he didn't know.

"No," he said.

"Are you sure?"

"Yes."

He kicked Olena in the stomach. She doubled over in pain. Cale bit down on his lip to stop from trying to bolt out of the chair.

"I'll ask again. Do you have Ivy in custody?"

Cale nodded. "Yes."

"Do you know where she is being held?"

"No."

Valentino obviously didn't like that answer because he hit Olena again. A cut opened up on her cheekbone, and a thin trickle of blood ran down to her jaw.

"I don't know where she is. She's in a safe house. But I don't know where."

Valentino stared at Cale for a minute then nodded. "I believe you."

Cale relaxed a little, but it was hard to see Olena hurt. He knew it looked worse than it was. She was a vampiress, and her healing powers were extraordinary. But knowing that didn't make it any easier to watch her being abused.

"Next question—where is the disc?"

"What disc?"

Valentino sighed. "Cale, I don't think you fully understand the rules I've set out." He nodded to the lycan holding Olena on her knees.

He yanked her up and dragged her toward the large wooden table. She struggled against his hold, kicking and raking her nails against his hands. Cale could see that she was hurting the lycan by the grimace on his face. Her captor nodded toward the other lycan, who had been standing in the corner motionless. He came over to help. He reached down and grabbed Olena's legs. She struggled even harder but it was to no avail. The two bruisers were much stronger than she was.

Cale knew what they were planning. He bucked in the chair violently. "Stop it! Stop! I don't know where the disc is. Ivy never told us where she hid it."

Valentino didn't respond but casually walked over to the table where Olena was being held down by the two lycans. Smiling, the witch withdrew a large dagger from a sheath that Cale hadn't seen hanging on his belt. The tip glittered in the low light. It had been dipped in silver.

Cale cursed so vehemently his throat grew ragged.

Valentino chuckled. "Ah, maybe you do understand the rules." But that didn't stop him. He cut open Olena's shirt, spreading the two sides. Cale could see her body flinch and jerk away from the tip of the knife.

"I've told you what I know."

"Maybe you have, maybe you haven't." Leaning over her, he lowered the knife to her chest. The tip touched her between her breasts. She screamed as the silver burned a mark into her flesh. Smoke curled up from the wound.

Rocking in his chair, Cale clenched his teeth. "I'm going to kill you. I'm going to kill you, you bastard."

"Does Interpol know about the virus?" He continued to cut her chest. She couldn't scream because one of the lycans had his hand over her mouth, but she bucked and writhed against the pain.

"Yes," Cale bit out between clenched teeth.

"Are they sending more agents?"

"No."

Valentino lifted the knife. "Do you love this woman?"

He looked at her for a long while before answering. Then it occurred to him that this had been by far the easiest question to answer. "Yes," he breathed out. "Yes, I love her."

"Does she love you?"

He shook his head. "I don't know."

"Well, we'll soon find out." Valentino waved his hand over Olena's writhing body.

A shimmer rushed through the air over her. The lycans let her go, and she rolled over onto her side. And that was when Cale saw her face shift and change. After several seconds, he realized she wasn't the love of his life but some anonymous woman. Valentino had used magic to transform this poor girl into Olena so he could torture the information out of him.

Valentino chuckled and sheathed his knife. "Lock him back up in the room. We'll soon find out how much Olena is willing to risk for him."

Chapter 26

Back at the lab, they were going over everything they were able to collect from the club and from Valentino's home. So far nothing was pointing to any one direction. François had told Olena it would take him some time to determine what kind of spell had been cast using Cale's cuff link.

Gabriel had talked to Otto, but the vampire couldn't tell him anything of consequence. He was still too distraught over the fact that Valentino may have murdered his lover. He swore up and down that he knew nothing about the virus that Ivy had created for Luc. If Valentino was part of some terrorist cell, Otto had no idea and not even suspicion. Nor could he help with Cale's whereabouts.

Olena loathed thinking about the possibility that there was nothing they could do to find Cale. Nothing but wait. For what, she wasn't sure, either. But she had a feeling Valentino was using Cale for leverage.

Sighing, she sank into the chair in Gabriel's office, feeling defeated and at a loss. When her cell phone shrilled from her jacket pocket, she slid it out and glanced at the incoming number. She didn't recognize it.

She flipped it open. "This is Olena."

"You've probably figured out by now that I put a spell on your dear little human."

It was Valentino. She waved at Gabriel to give her his pen and notepad. He handed them over quickly.

"What do you want?" She wrote down the phone number and handed it to Gabriel. He took it, picked up the phone on his desk and called it in. Maybe they could trace it.

"What I always want. Money, power, fame. A really good glass of wine."

"Is Agent Braxton still alive?"

"Of course. I'm not a murderous psychopath."

"That's debatable," she said, keeping a close eye on Gabriel's body language. She needed a sign that they could catch this guy. She wanted Cale back in her arms, safe and secure.

Valentino chuckled and it set the little hairs on her neck on edge. "Now, now, Olena, we mustn't be rude. You wouldn't want poor Cale to be harmed now, would you?" Another laugh. "Humans are so fragile, aren't they?"

"Yeah, they can be."

"He's in love with you, you know."

Olena's heart nearly stopped. She squeezed the phone tightly in her fist, tamping down the urge to beg Valentino to let Cale go.

"He's been moaning your name constantly. Pathetic if you ask me."

Gabriel held up his hand, indicating that they needed another three minutes to trace the number from Olena's cell phone.

"Well, I didn't ask you."

"No you didn't, did you?" He laughed again. "Now on to the reason I called. I want the girl and the disc delivered to me by 3:00 a.m. or your poor human Interpol agent is going for a dirt nap." He laughed even harder. "I always wanted to say that. Dirt nap. It's so amusing."

Olena glanced at her watch. It was nearly nine o'clock now, which meant they had only six hours. "It's not enough time. We have to find the girl first. Then the disc."

"Don't lie to me, Olena. I know you have the girl already."

"We need more time."

"Nope, sorry. I will call again in two hours with the address of the drop-off. If you lie to me again, Olena, I will send Cale back to you in pieces. Then you could bottle them and keep them forever. You see, who said humans couldn't last?"

"You know the department doesn't negotiate with terrorists."

"I know they won't. But will you? That's my question. How far will you go to save the man you love? I know you are a resourceful woman, Olena. I'm counting on that. And so is Cale." He hung up.

Gabriel shook his head at her. "We didn't get the trace."

She flipped her phone closed and slid it back into her pocket. "He's holding Cale for ransom. He wants the girl and the disc by 3:00 a.m."

Gabriel eyed her carefully. "You know we can't give Ivy and the virus to him."

"I know."

"Cale, more than anyone, knows that, too."

She knew he said it to make her feel less responsible, but she didn't really hear it. Guilt bubbled inside her. Deep down she knew it wasn't her fault but still she felt responsible. She should've been able to protect him from something like this.

It was ridiculous to think this way, especially since they both had high-risk jobs. Cale lived with the threat of death or capture every day working for Interpol. But it had happened in her city, by an Otherworlder. No amount of training could've protected Cale from this attack. She should've been able to.

She should've had François create some protective amulets for Cale. She hadn't been thinking straight. Along the way she'd forgotten that Cale was human, that he didn't have all the strength and power and protection that she had, that Gabriel had, that they all had. It was this mistake that might cost him his life.

Gabriel's voice broke into her thoughts. "This gives us six hours to find Cale's location."

She nodded, but her heart was not in it. It was aching too badly right now.

"We'll find him, Olena."

"I can't lose him, Gabriel. I just can't. I won't survive it."

He reached across the desk for her hand and squeezed it. She bit down on her lip to stop the tears. She wouldn't cry. She couldn't, not in front of Gabriel. But she sure did want to. To finally let out everything she'd been holding inside. Losing Cale would be losing everything. She wouldn't survive the heartbreak. Not this time.

Valentino knew she had deep feelings for Cale. That was why he'd called her. He was counting on her love for Cale. And the thing was, she wasn't sure she was going to disappoint him.

"I need to see Ivy."

"Why?"

"She said she would tell me where the disc is. We should get it to keep it safely out of other hands."

Gabriel looked at her for a few seconds. Olena could tell he was searching for the truth. He was good at reading people, but she was better at hiding. She'd been doing it a hell of a lot longer than he'd been alive.

He picked up the phone. "I'll have her brought in."

Olena nodded, and then stood. She needed to

move around. She was too jumpy, too nervous. She very well might have been setting up to go against all her morals and ethics, against an oath she took when she joined the team, to get back the man she loved.

Forty-five minutes later, Olena was standing in Luc Dubois's house, ripping it apart looking for the disc. Gabriel stood by, leaning on the counter. He'd understood why Olena needed to be the one to look for it, the one to find it.

Ivy was also there, watching as Olena rummaged through the freezer in the kitchen. The girl told her that was where Luc had hidden it. ICE in the ice box.

Except it wasn't there.

"It's not in here."

Frowning, Ivy rushed to her side. "It has to be."

Olena turned, showing the girl her hands full of crushed ice. She'd taken everything out and searched through all the bags of ice. There had been three.

"When did he put it in here?"

She shook her head. "I don't remember. I gave it to him a couple of days before he was killed."

Olena looked at Gabriel. "Valentino doesn't

have it, or he wouldn't be going through all of this. He'd just take it and run."

"Luc must've moved it. It has to be in this house somewhere," he said. "We've searched the club offices. It wasn't there."

Olena glanced at her watch. It was just after ten o'clock. They had barely five hours. "We need more help to search the house. It can't be done with just the two of us."

"Three of us," Ivy piped in. "I'll help."

Olena nodded to her.

Gabriel flipped open his cell phone. "I'll call in Sophie and Kellen."

Twenty minutes later, the five of them were each tearing apart a room in Luc's house. Olena had taken the master bedroom. She was systematically searching every inch of the room, starting in the far corner by the window. She'd opened up pillows, taken apart air vents, torn out the lining in every single drawer in the room. So far, she'd found nothing.

Time was running out. She could feel it ticking away in her head, and in her heart. They had to find the disc. *She* had to find it, though she was still at odds with what she was going to do with it. Without it, though, there wouldn't ever be a chance of getting Cale back alive. And a chance was all she wanted.

At the king-size bed, which had already been stripped when they'd found Luc's head on a pillow at the foot, Olena lifted the mattress and pushed it over. She searched underneath it, sliced open the bottom and felt along the seams. Nothing.

On edge, she took a step back and surveyed the destruction she'd caused. It looked like a tornado had whipped through the room, tearing at everything not nailed down. Sighing, she ran a hand over her face and through her hair. Fatigue was starting to settle in. She tried as hard as she could to rub it away. When she looked up again, her eyes settled on the big painting on the wall overhanging the bed.

It was an abstract, all dark sweeps of paint. It looked like a storm with black and grays and whites all swirling together into one massive ball of turmoil. Something about it interested her. As she drew closer to it, she could see the artist's name scrawled in the corner of the canvas in black letters. Ivy Seaborn.

Olena grabbed the painting and took it off the wall. She set it face down on the box spring.

Taking out her penknife, she cut along the sides, opening up the back, which had been covered in a beige, linenlike covering. She lifted it up. And there, pressed against the back of the painting, was the computer disc.

She peeled it off and held it up between her fingers. It wasn't very big, a smaller disc than a regular CD or DVD. She could slide it into her back pocket and no one would know. She could do that and when Valentino called she could tell him she had the disc and would trade it for Cale. She could save his life with this one little thing.

She sensed movement at the doorway and palmed the disc in her left hand. It was Gabriel.

"Did you find it?" he asked as he walked into the room.

She opened her mouth to say no when her cell phone shrilled again. She checked her watch. It was too early to be Valentino. She checked the number. It wasn't the same as last time, but that didn't necessarily mean anything. She flipped it open.

"This is Olena."

"Do you have the disc?"

She glanced at Gabriel, motioning with her

hand to get her something she could write with. "Yeah."

He handed her his notepad and a pen. The look in his eyes told her that he knew something was up. That she wasn't telling him everything. Taking the things he offered, she turned, giving him her back.

"Good," Valentino said. "I'm going to give you the address for the drop-off." He rattled off an obscure address she wasn't familiar with. She took it down. "Now I'm going to give you another address. If I tell you, can you memorize it without writing it down?"

"Yeah."

"Good. I knew I could count on you, Olena. I knew that Cale meant more to you than bureaucratic bullshit. You're a survivor, and you'll do what you have to. I like that about you."

She listened as he gave her another address and a time to meet. This location she knew. It was near the wharf. She kept still so as not to give anything away, then snapped her phone shut.

She turned around to look at Gabriel.

"Did he give you the address?"

"Yes." Then she handed the notebook and the disc over to Gabriel.

He kept her gaze as he accepted what she gave him. He nodded to her, and she knew he'd understood completely what she was giving him.

"Don't give up, Olena. This isn't over. We still have time to find him. Trust me."

With a slight nod, she left the room. She needed a private place to let go. She felt like she'd handed over her heart. She felt hollow inside. And she had no hope that the feeling would ever go away. Not in ten years, not in one hundred.

Chapter 27

Cale didn't know how long he'd been lying on his side on the floor in the small dark room. It could've been two hours or two days. Time was of little importance to him right now. He could barely think past the throbbing pain in his body and the sickness in his heart.

After being duped by Valentino's illusion, Cale had gone ballistic. He'd yanked on his ropes and managed to get one of his hands free. Bloody and raw, but free. He'd gotten halfway out of the chair before the two lycans pounced on him and beat him down again. He didn't care. He had one thing in his mind, and that was to rip Valentino apart for his twisted manipulations.

His soul had ripped in two as he watched Olena, or the woman he thought to be Olena, being tortured. And there was nothing he could do about it. He wasn't strong or quick enough to break his bonds and help her. In this world he was too weak. It hurt him so badly to not be able to do anything but watch like a helpless child.

If only he'd been stronger, faster, more aware of the Otherworld, then he wouldn't be in this mess. Olena wouldn't be out there wondering and worrying about him. He imagined she was likely going nuts trying to find him. Or at least in a small, selfish way, he hoped she was.

His back was to the door but he heard it open. Without looking he knew who had entered. The witch was a showman, and he wanted another audience to what he thought was his glorious plan.

Cale ignored him and didn't move. Although he wasn't sure he could move even if he wanted to, not after a couple of broken ribs, a broken nose, ruptured blood vessels in his eyes, and a plethora of cuts and bruises. He was a bloody wreck. But given the right opportunity, he'd muster enough energy and strength to take down his captors and get the hell out of Dodge.

Valentino moved into the room. Cale could sense him standing over him, probably leering like the vulture he was. "What do you want?"

"To inform you that you'll soon be reunited with your vampiress lover."

"Really? I somehow doubt that."

He chuckled. "Don't pout, Agent Braxton, it's very unbecoming."

"Screw you."

"No, thank you. You're really not my type. I like my men stronger, less human."

Cale didn't respond. There was no point in bantering with the witch. He was one of those people off whom insults just bounced. A sociopath, through and through.

"Oh, don't be so glum. Once I have the virus, I'll let you go. I'll have no further use for you."

Cale smirked. "You won't let me go. You know I'll be after you. You know that Interpol will put everything they've got into tracking you down. They aren't going to let a potential threat to international safety like the ICE virus just up and walk away."

That made Valentino laugh, and he clapped his

hands together. "Oh, yeah. You got me. I am lying to you. You're right. I am going to kill you."

Cale rolled over and glared up at Valentino. "Then why don't you get it over with?"

"Because I'm having way too much fun watching you suffer. You're probably wondering and hoping that the cavalry will come to rescue you. That sweet, darling, sexy Olena comes rushing in, fists flying, to sweep you up in her arms and carry you off into the sunset." He moved his gaze from Cale and glanced around the room. "Even if by chance they did find this place, I've set so many traps that no one will get out alive."

Looking away was Valentino's second mistake. Taunting Cale about Olena had been his first.

Faster than he thought he could move with his injuries, Cale swept his legs forward and knocked Valentino's legs out from under him. Cale was up and on top of Valentino in seconds. He had his knee pressed against the witch's throat, leaning on it hard, using all his weight to crush his windpipe.

"You should've killed me, asshole, instead of just talking about it."

Valentino struggled underneath him, pummeling his leg and side with his hands. But Cale held on, pushing even more with his leg. But his victory didn't last long.

The two lycans burst into the room. Before Cale could react, one of them kicked him in the head, sending him reeling across the room to land in a heap against the far wall. Blood coated his throat. He could feel it pouring down from his nose and his mouth. The sensation lasted only a second more before he promptly and mercifully passed out.

Chapter 28

Olena felt raw and worn-out when she got back to the lab. Gabriel hadn't said a word to her on the car ride back. He must've sensed her need for silence, for privacy. She appreciated the fact that he hadn't given her an ethics speech on what could have happened, what she had been planning.

She really didn't need him to remind her that she was possibly giving up the love of her life for what was right. However right it was, she didn't want to hear it. Her wounded soul couldn't bear it.

As she walked down the hallway, she stopped at one of the vending machines and bought a bottle of blood. She needed the energy and the nutrients if she was going to stay on her feet.

Just as she twisted the cap, François popped his head out of his lab. "*Mon coeur,* I have something for you."

Taking her drink with her, she went to see what he had. Olena watched as François carefully plucked the cuff link she'd found at Phantasia—the only evidence they had of Cale's disappearance—out of a liquid solution and set it on a drying sheet on the counter.

"I did a bunch of tests."

"Anything odd in the spell?"

The witch had finished analyzing the residual substances left on the cufflink. All magic left some sort of imprint, either chemical, physical or spiritual. François could sense all three. He was one of the best magical analyzers in the world.

"There are several spells on this. Lemon juice, sea salt for a dream spell, residue of a black thread, probably used for a binding, lavender and cypress, used most often in a sleep potion. I also sense Merlin Oil, which is made with hazelnut oil and fir oil on this, most often used for a type of transportation spell. All these elements are available at any magical shop."

"So nothing to determine where Valentino may have conjured these spells?"

He tapped his lips with his finger. "Well, there was one thing I found a little bit odd. I found glasswort, which is a plant that grows along the water's edge, used in making glass, but it also makes a really good binding spell."

"Why is it odd?"

"Because it's not something witches use often. There are better and more easily obtainable plants at anyone's disposal. I've never heard of any shop carrying glasswort in its inventory."

"So, this would be what, like a signature ingredient? Possibly only used by one certain witch?"

He nodded. "Yeah, could be. Also, could be that the plant is nearby so it's easy to use. Could be that the element is part of the spell."

"In what way?"

"Like a location. Especially when a transportation spell is added to it."

"Which means wherever the plant came from could be where Cale was transported to?"

François nodded. "Yes, that very well could be the case."

Elated at having found something she could use, Olena leaned over and kissed François on the cheek. "Thank you, darling."

He smiled at her. "Anything for you, *mon coeur.*"

She turned to leave, wanting to find Gabriel to tell him what François discovered.

"I hope it helps you find him, Olena."

She stopped to smile at François. "Me, too."

He shrugged. "If you like him this much, then he must be an okay guy."

She nodded, and then left to rush down the hall to Gabriel's office. She didn't knock but burst in. He was at his desk on the phone.

"I have something." He put up his finger to tell her to give him a minute, then finished his call. Once he hung up, she was talking again. "François found an unusual plant substance in one of the spells on the cuff link."

"Okay."

"It grows only on the edge of waterways."

His eyebrows went up. "Like a river."

"Exactly. François said that Valentino may have used it because it was readily available and because it might've triggered Cale to be transported to where it is."

"You're thinking the warehouse district, down by the wharf?"

She nodded. "It would be a logical place. Most of the buildings are empty, there's no traffic down there anymore, and it's fairly close to the downtown where the club is situated."

"All right. That gives us something to go on. We could get a few units down there to check."

She glanced at her watch. "We have three hours until the scheduled drop-off."

"That'll give us time, but we'll have to do recon on the wharf quickly and quietly. If Valentino suspects we've found him…"

He left the rest unsaid. He didn't have to voice it. Olena knew what it meant. If Valentino suspected, he'd kill Cale instantly. They were taking a big risk, but Olena felt it was worth it. It was their one and only shot to get Cale out alive.

"I'll call it in. We'll get three groups organized to do a grid search on the wharf. We'll coordinate it from outside the area." He picked up the phone. "We should also get the drop-off team together. We don't want to tip Valentino off. You should consider keeping up the ruse as well. If he thinks that you're really going to go through with the switch, there's more of a chance he'll keep Cale alive. Until he has what he wants. But by then, we'll have him."

"I want to be there for the takedown. I have to be there when we find Cale."

Gabriel nodded. "I understand, Olena, but maybe that wouldn't be for the best. Besides, you need to be at your drop-off."

She rubbed a hand over her face again. As the hours ticked off, she was finding it harder and harder to think straight. She wasn't sure if they could find Cale. Sighing, she sat back in the chair and stared up at the ceiling, searching for a way to be in two places at once.

She bolted forward. "An illusion spell. François could do one easily."

Gabriel set down the phone and rubbed his cheek. She could tell he was thinking hard.

"Valentino won't be the one that comes to the drop-off, I'm sure of that. He won't risk being out in the open. He'll send someone to the pick-up. No one will know."

"Who do we send?"

"How about Sophie? I trust her more than anyone else."

"Okay, talk to Sophie and see if she's willing to do it. Hopefully we won't even need to go through with it."

She hoped so as well. More than she'd ever hoped before. She stood and marched out of the room to track Sophie down and set the plan in motion. It wouldn't be long before it was all over. One way or another.

Chapter 29

An hour later the team was set up just a few blocks west of the warehouse district down by the river. They set up shop above an old pawnshop. Gabriel had sent out three two-man teams to search the area for any possible sign of Cale's location. It was down to the wire. Only two hours to go and counting.

Unable to sit still, Olena paced the small room set up as the command center. She needed to do something, anything, to keep busy or she felt she'd explode.

"Olena, go for a walk or something," Gabriel

suggested from his seat at the window. A handheld radio was set on the table by his coffee cup, ready for the teams to call in.

She whirled on him, about to give him a piece of her mind, when Sophie jumped to the rescue. She set her hand on Olena's shoulder.

"I'll go with you. We'll get some fresh air."

Together they walked out into the cool early morning. Even down here, at one in the morning, there was something going on. Nouveau Monde never slept. It was what happened when at least one third of the population was just starting their day.

Olena rubbed her arms, but she wasn't cold. She was afraid. Afraid that they wouldn't find Cale in time. Afraid she'd missed out on finding happiness.

Sophie must've picked up on her feelings. She put her arm around Olena. "It's going to be okay."

She nodded to Sophie, but she wasn't so sure. "How did you get through not knowing if Kellen was alive or…" She couldn't finish the sentence.

"One minute at a time. If I could get through that minute, I knew I could get through the next." She shrugged. "I dove into work. I kept my mind busy. Anything not to have to think about it."

"Bet you thought about it, anyway."

Sophie nodded. "Twenty-four seven."

Olena took in a deep breath of cool air, then let it out. "I'm going to kill Valentino when we find him."

Sophie hugged her tight. "I know."

The door behind them opened, and Gabriel poked his head out. "We may have found where they're holding Cale."

They all went back upstairs, and Gabriel told them that one of the teams had found two big, beefy lycans going in and out of a large, seemingly abandoned warehouse and a lot of residual magic. One of the team members was a witch. She could see the faint red haze of spell casting around the building.

"When do we go in?" Olena asked.

"Olena—" Gabriel started.

"Don't say it. I'm going, and that's the end of it. No one is going to stop me. And if they try, I will hurt them. You have my promise on that."

Gabriel cleared his throat to start again. "I was just going to say that you should hang back in the second line and let the front line clear the area."

She nodded. "Fine. I can do that."

"Okay. Let's get our guy back."

Fifteen minutes later, Olena was impatiently waiting behind a line of four officers outfitted in black SWAT gear. They were the first line and were to go in, smoke out the place and take down the bad guys. Then Olena could go in and search for Cale.

She told Gabriel she would wait, but the longer she thought about it, the more she knew she couldn't. She had to go in first. She had to be the one to find him.

On a count of three, the four officers ran toward the warehouse to form a perimeter. She watched, her hands shaking, sweat slicking her back, as they mounted their assault. Five seconds later, they simultaneously lobbed smoke canisters through the windows. And that was when all hell broke loose.

There were shouts and shots fired and explosions of color all around the warehouse. It was obvious the place was rigged with varying types of traps, one of them magic. Who knew what kind of spells were being triggered as the team moved in?

She couldn't hold back. She had to get in there. What if Cale was killed in the crossfire?

Olena set out toward the warehouse. Gabriel

called her back, but she ignored him and kept on moving. She ran to the first checkpoint, a rusted-out old car to hide behind. As she scouted out the situation, she unholstered her weapon and flipped off the safety. On the count of three, she ran toward the warehouse, where more shots and shouts rang out. It sounded like a war zone in there.

Right before she reached the back-door entrance, she paused. Something wasn't right. A sense of dread and wrongness washed over her. Sensing something creep over her back, she looked up, searching for the cause of her unease. That was when she met Valentino's gaze from the next building over. He was staring at her from the top floor of what looked an old factory.

They had the wrong building.

Olena clicked on the radio that was attached to the collar of her crime-scene jacket as she ran full out toward the next building. "We have the wrong building! Get out! Cale is not in there. He's in the next building over to the east."

She made it to the large bay door of the next building and kicked it open. Without hesitation she entered, weapon pointed. It didn't matter what they threw at her, she was bulletproof, and because of the amulct François had given her before she left, magic-proof as well.

"Cale!" she yelled the second she was in the building. She crossed the empty main floor to the metal staircase. "Cale!"

She took the stairs two at a time, and reached the next floor in seconds. There was a long hallway with what looked like offices to her right. Valentino was that way. She was sure of it.

She edged along the wall, careful to step over the debris on the floor. When she reached one of the offices, she looked through the dirty window, then drew her head back again. It was empty. She quickly passed the door and then kept walking to the next office.

Before she could reach the door, Valentino stepped out with a sardonic grin on his face. "Well, well, you are full of surprises."

She trained her gun on him. "Where is Cale?"

"You know, I had you pegged all wrong. I thought you were an opportunist. I thought you were a survivor. A woman who would do anything to get what she wanted."

"I am. And I will." The weapon never wavered in her hand. "If you tell me where he is, I might let you live."

He motioned toward the room he'd just stepped out of. "He's in there."

Cautiously, Olena moved forward, keeping her gun trained on Valentino. He took a step back to allow her entrance into the room. She kept her gaze on the witch as she sidestepped into the room. Cale was there in the middle of the room, chained to a chair, tape over his mouth. He looked badly beat-up, but he was alive. He blinked up at her, his eyes wide in surprise at seeing her.

Relief surged through her. "I found you. Oh my love, I found you." She moved toward him, intending to untie him, when Valentino started to laugh.

Startled, she whipped around to glare at him. He looked way too happy for a man who'd just been caught.

Chapter 30

Cale startled awake from his spot on the floor. He hadn't moved since being kicked across the room. He struggled to sit up and leaned his back against the wall. He could hear gunshots ringing out from nearby. He turned his head, pressing his ear to the wall. The shots were definitely outside, near the building he was in. Maybe the cavalry had actually arrived.

He had to be ready. He couldn't just sit here, broken and unable to aid in his own rescue. He wanted to see Olena again on his feet and not on his back. Mustering all his strength, Cale pushed up with his legs, using the wall as leverage. At first he wobbled and nearly fell, but he braced his hands on the wall and kept his feet.

He had to take in a few breaths before he could even think about walking across the room to the door. His head was swimming in a thick gray fog. His vision ebbed in and out. And it wouldn't take much for him to lose his lunch. Every movement he made sent his gut rolling. Pain was a constant, unwelcome companion.

But he had to suck it up if he was going to get the hell out of this room and find Olena.

Shaking his head and rubbing a hand over his face to clear the sweat from his eyes, Cale pushed off the wall and stumbled toward the door.

He made it without falling onto his face. Leaning against the door, he took in some more deep breaths. His lungs spasmed with every motion. He suspected one of his broken ribs had punctured something inside. It probably wouldn't be long before he started coughing up blood. If only he had the rejuvenation powers of an Otherworlder.

He was about to try the doorknob again when the door swung open and one of the lycan bruisers stomped into the room. Surprised, he swung around toward Cale, but he came too late. Cale was already in motion.

Cale kicked the mammoth between the legs with a crunching blow. The lycan doubled over, and Cale chopped him in the throat with the side of his hand. The two blows wouldn't kill the giant, but at least they would afford Cale enough time to get out of the room and hopefully stumble his way into his rescuers' hands.

Without looking back to see if the lycan was up and after him, Cale moved as fast as he could down a corridor. It was a now-or-never scenario.

There were rooms on either side of him as he stumbled forward. Rooms that looked like offices. He was in some sort of abandoned shipping warehouse. Probably by the water, by the musty smell in the air.

He kept moving, putting one foot in front of the other. He needed a weapon of some sort. It wouldn't be long before the lycan was after him. Nothing short of a bullet in the head was going to put the bruiser down.

Cale scanned the floor as he moved, looking for anything he could use. A pipe, a broken piece of lumber. But nothing jumped out at him.

Risking a glance behind him, Cale rounded a

corner. The lycan wasn't on his ass. In fact, he appeared to be pretty much alone. Except for the gunshots he could still hear in the distance. Then he heard something else that gave him pause. A voice. A beautiful, Russian-accented voice that nearly made him weep with joy.

He came up short and peered into one of the offices. And that's when he saw her. His gorgeous vampiress. She was bent over talking to another man, who was bound to a chair. Another man that looked exactly like him.

He stepped into the room. "Olena?"

She whirled around, confusion furrowing her brow. She looked at him, then at his doppelganger in the chair, then back to him. "What the hell?"

"That guy isn't me, Olena." He pointed at the struggling man in the chair. "It's an illusion. It's a trick."

Valentino stepped out of the shadows. Cale hadn't seen him when he'd first entered the room. He was smiling. "Isn't this fun? Who's who in the zoo?"

Cale moved toward Olena. "Look at me, luv. It's really me."

She searched his face for a long moment, and then something in her gaze told him that she knew it was truly him. A grin split her face. She turned toward him, her arms open, and he moved toward her.

That was when he saw movement behind her. Whoever had been bound to the chair miraculously stood up. He had a metal stake in his hand and he was advancing toward Olena.

Cale rushed to her, grabbed her by the arms and spun her out of the way. He twisted around and felt something pinch him in the back. He didn't feel any pain. He was just relieved to have gotten Olena out of the way.

Everything seemed to move in slow motion after that.

He heard Valentino laughing, but his voice sounded far off, from a distance. He saw Olena's eyes widen and her mouth form a surprised O. He saw a flash of anguish come over her face. Why was she so sad? They were together again. She should've been happy.

"Cale!" She bounded toward him, her arms outstretched trying to grab him. He didn't feel like he'd been falling, but Olena caught him and brought him down to the floor. Then she disappeared in a blur of motion.

In the next second, Cale felt a spray of

moisture on his face. He looked around to see what had been his body double collapse onto the floor in a blur of blood. The moment the body hit the wood, it transformed into one of the lycan henchmen. Valentino had used him as bait to hurt Olena. But Cale had saved her. He smiled, knowing that he'd pushed her out of harm's way.

Valentino took that opportunity to move toward the door to escape.

"Stop him, Olena," he said, his voice sounding hollow in his ears. "He's getting away."

Before he could blink, she was on Valentino. She had him dangling by the neck with one hand.

The witch was tearing at her hand and kicking at her stomach, but it didn't look like it was having any effect on her.

"I told you I was going to kill you, Valentino," she snarled.

Cale had never seen her like that before. Her eyes glowed a bright green, and her fangs were fully distended. She was snarling, fierce as a wild animal.

"But I'm not going to." She tossed him to the side. He hit the wall hard and promptly slid down like a rag doll onto the floor. "You can rot in a jail cell for the rest of your life instead."

She returned to Cale's side, wrapping her arms around him and cradling his body, pressing her hands on his back. "I'm here, Cale. I'm here." Tears rolled down her cheeks.

He rubbed them away with his fingers. "Why the tears? We won. We got the bad guys."

Pursing her lips, her gaze fell to his side, then up again. He looked down, following her eyes. He was covered in blood. Beneath him was a widening pool that seemed to have no end.

He looked up at her face. Her eyes were so beautiful, even swimming in tears. He smiled and traced her lips with this thumb. "You're so beautiful. I love to look at you."

"Hush. Don't talk. Help is coming."

"I knew you would come for me."

"Always."

His eyelids felt heavy. He was having a difficult time keeping them open. But he wanted to. He wanted to keep looking at Olena. He never wanted to lose her image in his mind.

The rest of the team swarmed into the room, Gabriel in the lead. He came over to where Cale lay and knelt down on the other side of him.

"How is he?"

Olena didn't speak. She just shook her head.

Gabriel lifted Cale up a little and looked down at his back. His face visibly paled. It was then that Cale knew he was dying. He'd taken the mortal wound meant for Olena. The look that passed between Gabriel and Olena spoke volumes.

"Can you do anything?" she asked.

Gabriel swallowed. Cale watched the motion in his throat. Then the lycan shook his head.

Cale cradled Olena's face. "It's okay. I'm not in any pain."

Sobbing, she leaned down and pressed her lips to his. "I can't stand to lose you."

"Me, either. I don't want to leave you."

"I love you, Cale."

He smiled and kissed her, breathing in her smell, inhaling everything about her. He'd longed to hear those words from her. And now he had them. "I love you."

Closing her eyes, Olena lifted her head to the sky and screamed. Cale's body shook from the violence of it. He could hear her pain and her anguish. He felt the same inside. He didn't want to leave after just having found her again. Anger at the injustice made him shudder.

She came forward again, and her eyes were glowing. "I won't let you go."

"Olena," Gabriel said, a warning in his voice.

"Tell me it's okay, and I won't let you go."

At first Cale didn't understand what she was saying. But the fierceness in her gaze and the way she was breathing, her fangs overhanging her bottom lip, tipped him off. She wanted to turn him.

"I can keep death away. I can turn you and you'll never feel death's knock again."

"Olena, you don't know what will happen."

"Stay out of this, Gabriel. It's Cale's decision."

The warmth of his body was draining out of him. He knew it wouldn't be long now before death stole him for good. But he didn't have to go. Not really. He could cheat death's embrace and stay with Olena for eternity. To love her for a lifetime. It seemed like a fantasy and nothing more. But it was true. He could have everything he'd ever wanted from this woman. All he had to do was say yes.

He looked up into Olena's face and saw what he needed to see. She loved him, mind, body and soul. He could see it in the glow of her emerald-green eyes. Here was his answer, staring at him, begging him to let her love him for a lifetime.

He ran his thumb over her lips one last time,

the tip of this thumb rubbing the edge of her fangs. "Yes. I want to live. I want to be with you forever."

Olena leaned forward and tilted his head back, then she bit into his neck. The sharp pain radiated up his neck and seemed to settle in his head. Soon everything faded into black, into nothingness. Then Cale died.

Chapter 31

For three days and three nights Olena watched over Cale.

After she'd drained him of what little blood he had left, on the hard floor of the abandoned warehouse, she'd torn at her own wrist and dribbled her blood into his mouth. She'd massaged his throat to help him swallow it down. He had, and then had fallen into a deep state of unconsciousness, much like a coma.

The main thing was that he hadn't died.

She'd had the paramedics, who'd finally showed two minutes after she'd bled him dry, transport him to her house. She'd set him up in her bedroom, making him as comfortable as she could. She made the room dark and cool and conducive to healing.

He hadn't fully awakened yet. He'd come to once, violent, out of his mind and ravenous for blood. She'd fed him, again helping him swallow every mouthful. Then he'd fallen back into unconsciousness.

She couldn't deny she was worried, but she wasn't letting it swallow her up. She wouldn't let it destroy her faith. Faith that Cale would rise up soon. A vampire and hers for an eternity.

Olena went into the kitchen to make herself a salad. Marie jumped up onto the counter and meowed. Purring, she rubbed her sleek body against Olena's arm. Olena scratched her on top of the head.

"What are you doing, my little girl?"

The cat meowed and swished her tail toward the bedroom.

Olena smiled. "Yeah, I am worried for him as well."

Just then her phone rang. She snatched it up after two rings. "Hello."

"How's he doing?" It was Gabriel.

"No change yet. But I'm hopeful."

He didn't respond. He knew as well as she did that the longer he remained in the coma, the worse his chances. After five days, the chances that Cale would survive became slim to none. Turning was a very hard thing to do, and the odds of survival were a grim one in ten thousand, which was one of the reasons she'd never considered turning anyone before. It was like watching the one you loved die twice without hope of helping them.

Olena had done all she could to aid Cale's transition. Now it was up to fate to play its hand.

"Ivy was asking after you."

She smiled thinking of the teen witch. "Was she? Is she all settled yet?"

"Not yet. But she will be soon. She has one last meeting with the lawyers, then she's a free bird."

After Valentino was taken into custody, the whole case just blew open. They found evidence linking Valentino to Luc's murder. His prints were on one of the glasses they'd found in the basement. And they'd found one of Valentino's hairs in the bedroom near Luc Dubois's severed head. He'd been the one to decapitate the vampire.

They had Ivy safely tucked away, as well as the

virus. Both were secure and out of Valentino's hands. They had yet to find the terrorists who'd been willing to pay for the virus, but Olena had confidence that eventually Interpol would.

She'd met Cale's boss, and he seemed like a caring and determined man. Once he found out about Cale and the entire case, he'd assigned ten agents to track down the terrorists.

"Do you need anything?" Gabriel asked.

She smiled. Her boss was a generous soul when he wanted to be. Most of the time he was a taskmaster and a tyrant. "No. I'm okay."

"Call with any changes."

"I will." She paused, then said, "Thank you, Gabriel."

"You're welcome. I'm here if you need me."

She hung up the phone, feeling maudlin. The reality of the situation just seemed to crash in on her. In two days, Cale could be gone for good. Forever. And she'd never be able to get him back.

Sighing deeply, she returned to her mundane task of making a salad. She had to eat, and it was something to do. She grabbed the vinaigrette from the refrigerator. When something jabbed her in the gut.

She dropped the salad dressing and rubbed a

hand over her belly. Something had changed. Something remarkable.

She whipped around to see Cale, rumpled and disheveled, his hair sticking up every which way, standing in the kitchen doorway. He wore nothing but a pair of black boxer shorts and damn if he didn't look sexy as hell. Her knees buckled and she nearly collapsed onto the floor.

"I'm hungry. Got anything to eat in here?"

She didn't hesitate. She crossed the floor and buried herself in the warmth of his body, wrapping her arms tightly around him. Chuckling, he returned the gesture, squeezing her close. He settled his face into her hair and breathed in deeply.

"You smell like ecstasy."

She laughed and squeezed him tight. "How do you feel?"

"Good. Hungry, though. My stomach's growling like a bear."

"You'll feel that way for a while. You'll drink and eat but you won't feel satisfied. Not for a while, anyway."

"I also have a wicked boner."

She laughed even harder, very well aware of his erection pressing against her. "That'll take a while to sate as well."

"Is that so?" He ran his hands down her back to cup her rear end.

A rush of desire spread through her. It was hot and heavy and ferocious. She'd been waiting so long for him, she could barely contain the passion inside.

With no effort, Cale picked her up and set her down on the kitchen counter. He settled himself in between her legs and ran his tongue along her jawline.

Moaning, she let her head fall back. It hit the cupboard behind her but she didn't care. Cale was here, alive, and in her arms.

"Mmm, your skin tastes like vanilla. Your smell is intoxicating. My senses are in overdrive. It's like seeing and smelling and tasting for the first time." He nuzzled his nose into the crook of her neck just underneath the fall of her hair.

"It doesn't bother you?"

"What?" He licked the lobe of her ear.

"That you're a vampire now. Forever."

He leaned back and looked into her eyes. He smiled. "I'm exactly where I want to be. I'm exactly who I want to be. I love you, Olena. That will never change." Cupping her face with the palms of his hands, he tilted her head up to meet his lips. He covered her mouth with his, and Olena felt like her heart had exploded. His vampire kiss felt good. And right. And forever.

* * * * *

1010/89

Coming next month

THE VAMPIRE AFFAIR by Livia Reasoner

The world knew Michael Brandt as a playboy tycoon. The underworld knew him as a fierce vampire hunter. Then tabloid reporter Jessie Morgan uncovered his secret and Michael must fight heaven and hell to protect her from the power of the undead.

WOLFTRAP by Linda Thomas-Sundstrom

When a full moon awakens the beast within Dr Parker Madison, he is hell-bent on finding explanations for his new Otherworld form and his insatiable lust. Then he saves Chloe, the girl who stirs his darkest desires and may hold the answers he's searching for.

SINS OF THE HEART by Eve Silver

Soul reaper Dagan is on a quest to find his brother's remains and to find those responsible for his death. Roxy Tam is searching for the same thing but for different reasons. When Dagan and Roxy come together for a common goal, they must choose between honour and the inescapable passion that binds them…

On sale 5th November 2010

Available at WHSmith, Tesco, ASDA, Eason and all good bookshops.
For full Mills & Boon range including eBooks visit
www.millsandboon.co.uk